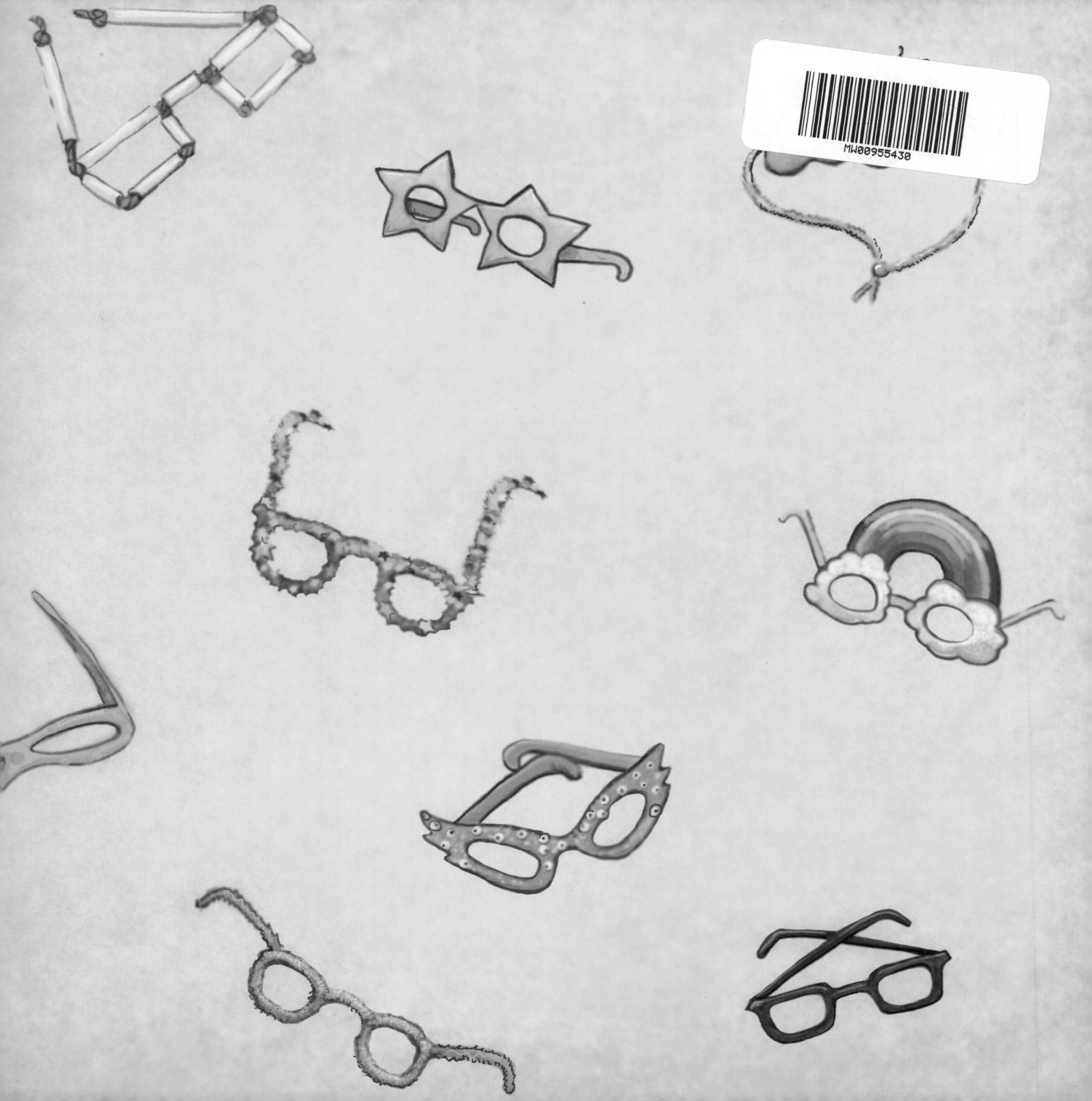

Carla's Glasses

Written by
Debbie Herman

Illustrated by
Sheila Bailey

FLASHLIGHT PRESS

To my SPEC-tacular family! Love you all! —DH

To my poet brother, Steve, who writes in a small room
in a tiny cabin beneath the singing pines. —SB

Thanks to my eye experts: Chana Lieber, Stacy Olswang, Linda Weil, and Kayla Cornelius.
And to Eye Spy Optical for their funky-frames inspiration. -DH

First Edition – September 2024

Cataloging-in-Publication data is available from the Library of Congress

Hardcover ISBN 9781947277717 • Ebook editions ISBN 9781947277724

Editor: Shari Dash Greenspan
Graphic Design: The Virtual Paintbrush

This book was typeset in Hanna.
Illustrations were rendered using a combination of watercolor and digital media.

Distributed by IPG • ipgbook.com

Flashlight Press • 527 Empire Blvd. • Brooklyn, NY 11225
FlashlightPress.com

**Flash
Light** PRESS

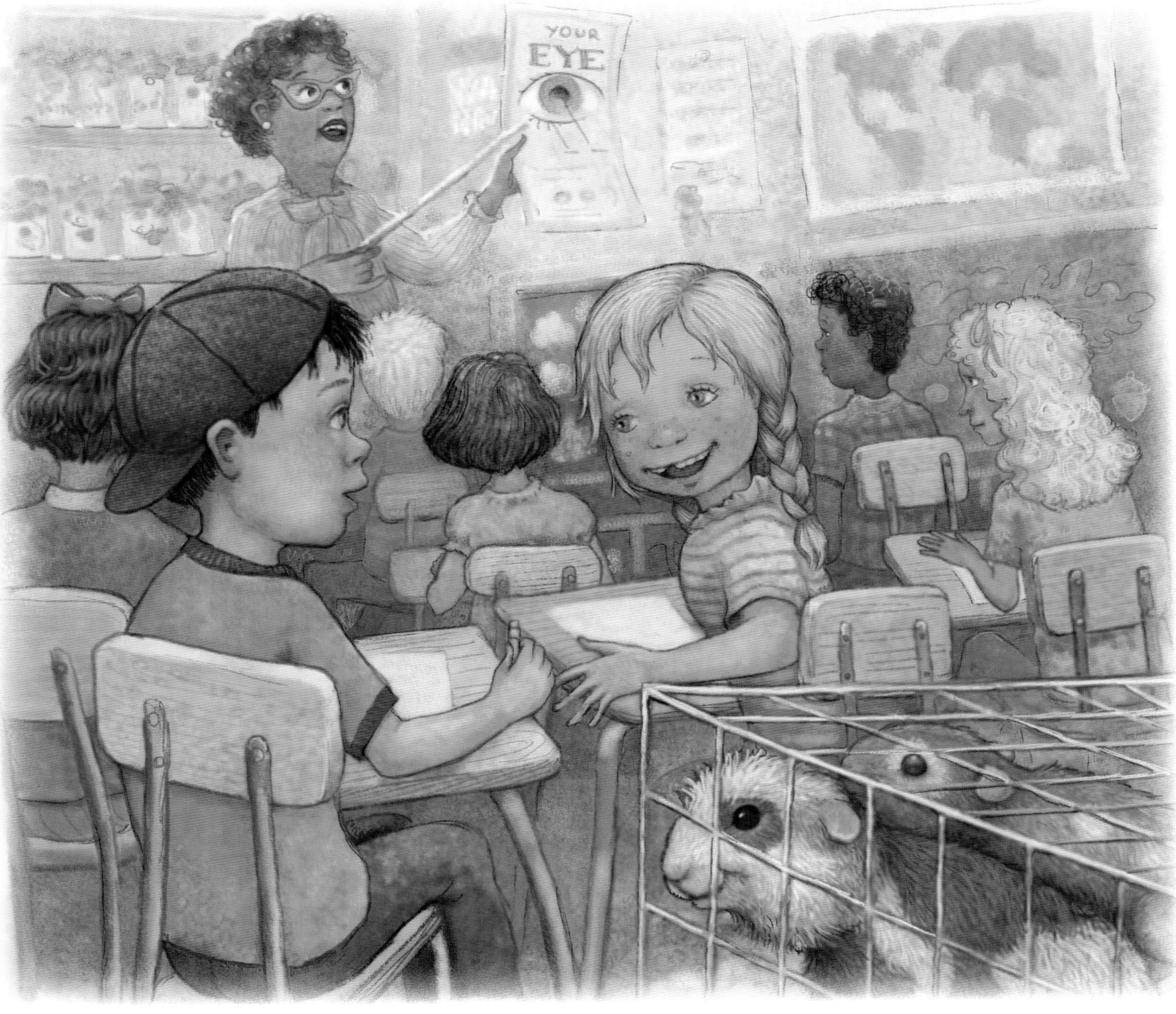
YOUR
EYE

On Monday, Ms. Pimento made an announcement. "A week from today is Vision Screening Day. The nurse will be checking everyone's eyesight."

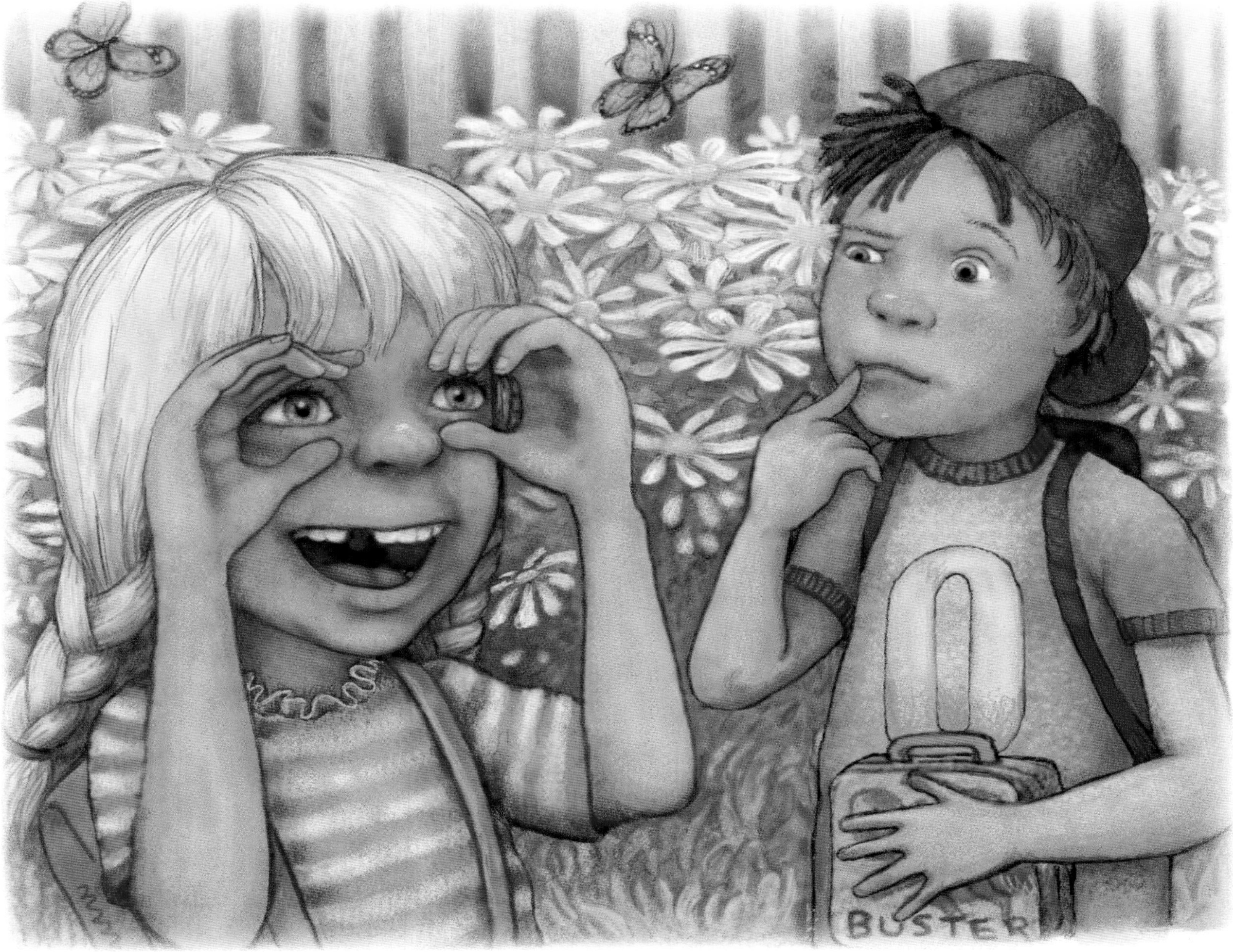
BUSTER

"I can't wait till next Monday!" said Carla to Buster as they walked home.
"Why?" he asked.
"Maybe I'll need glasses! Then I'll be the only kid in class to have them!"
"That's so YOU," said Buster. "You like to be different."

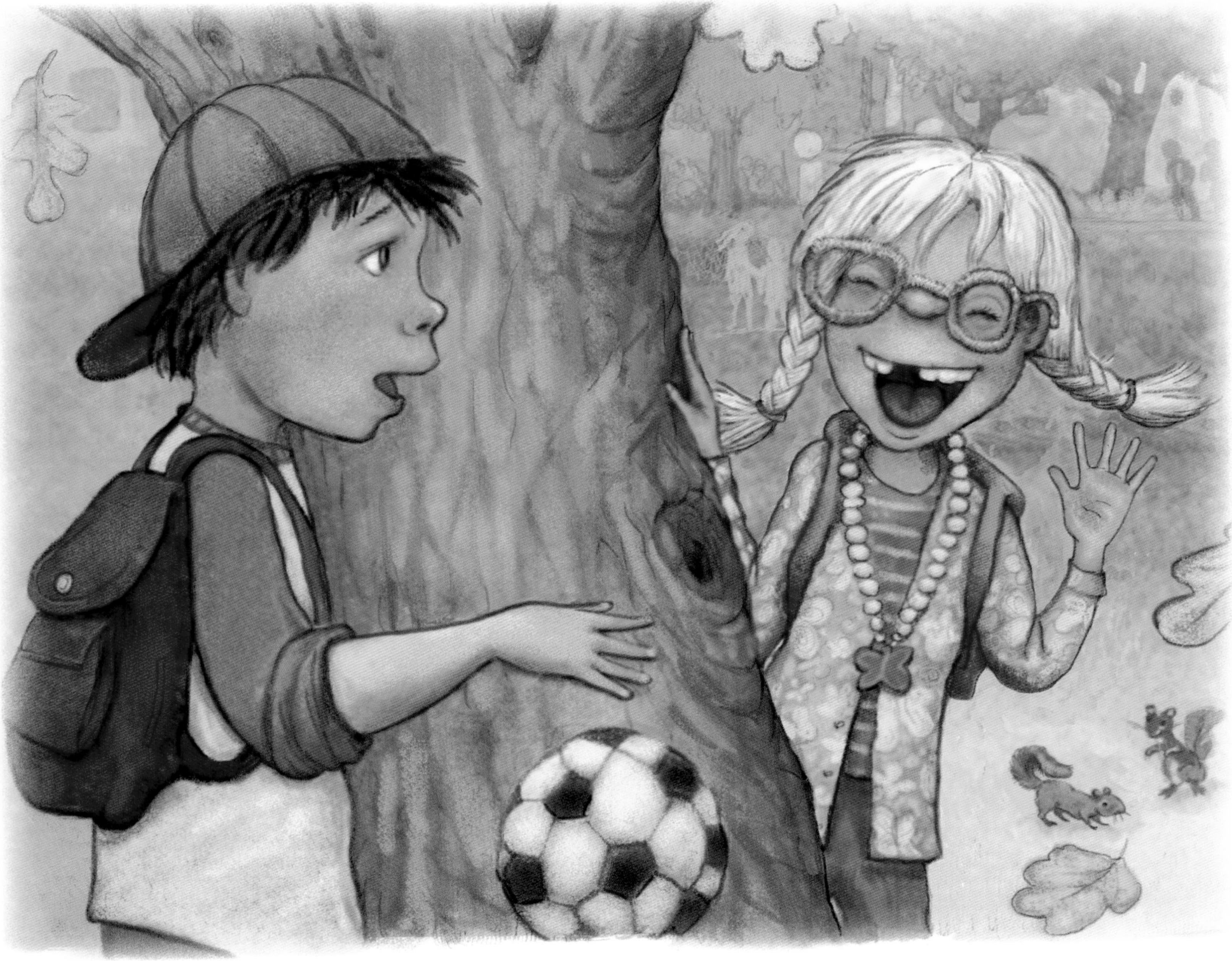

On Tuesday, Carla was wearing something unusual on her face. It was purple and fuzzy.
"What's with the pipe cleaners?" asked Buster.
"They're eyeglass frames," said Carla. "I made them myself. I'm trying to see what colors and styles look good on me for when I get real glasses. What do you think of them?"
"I think they look like pipe cleaners," said Buster.

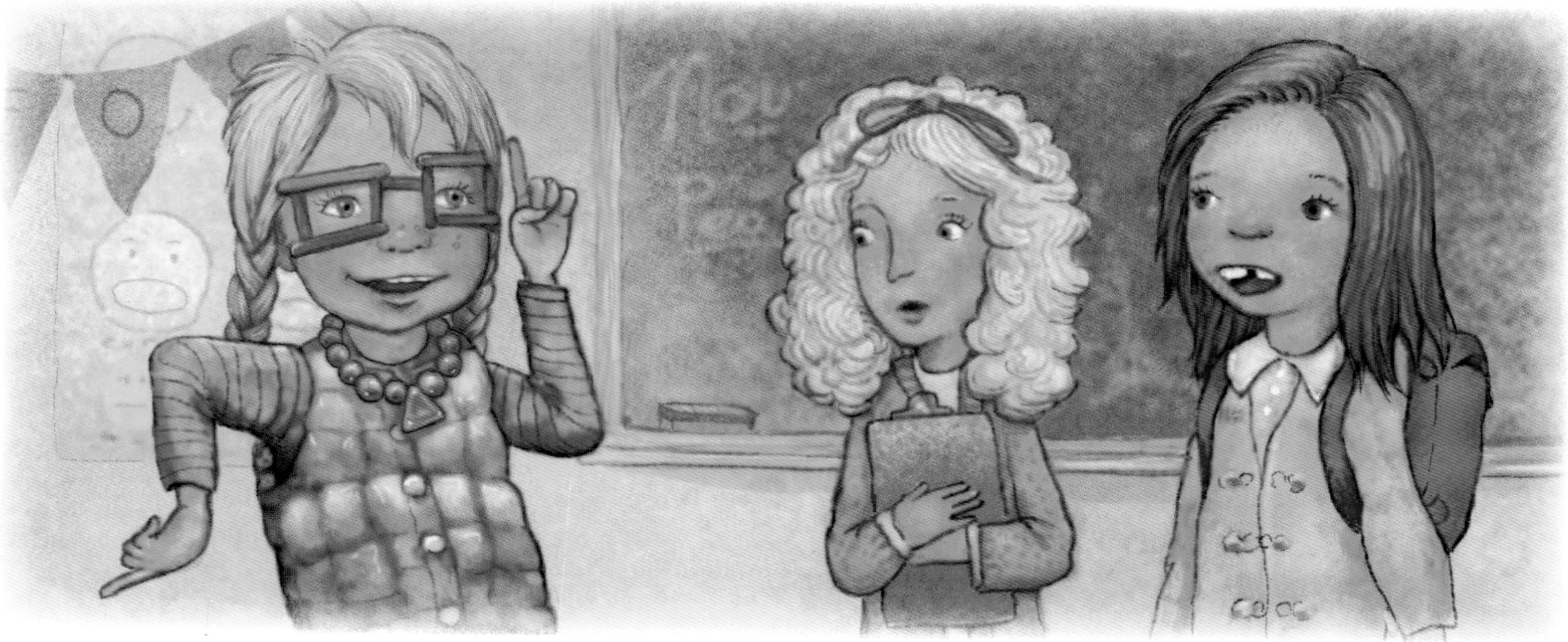

On Wednesday, Carla's glasses were square and made of craft sticks. "Do these frames flatter my features?" she asked Lottie and Leslie.

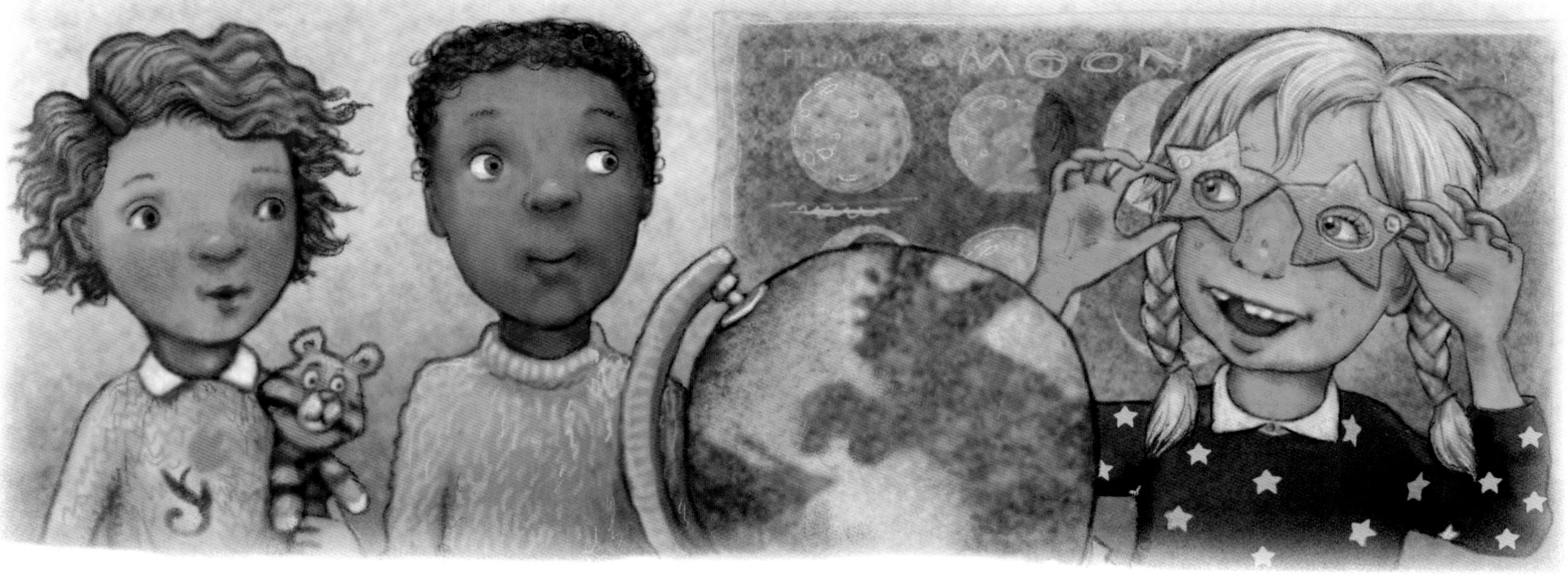
MOON

On Thursday, Carla's glasses were star-shaped and made of construction paper. "This pair really accentuates my eyes," she said to Darcy and Marcus.

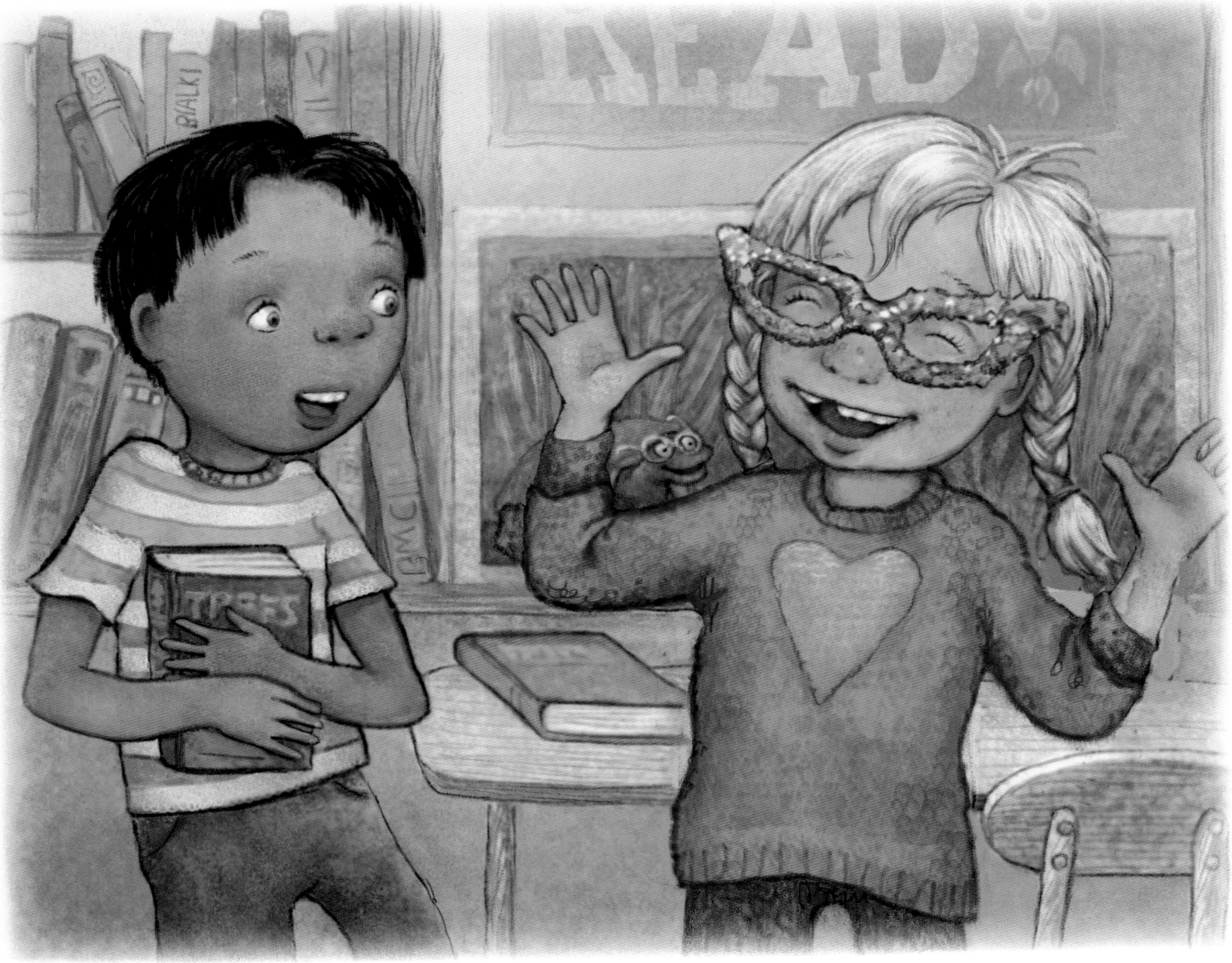
BIALKI
TREES

On Friday, Carla's glasses were shaped like cats' eyes and covered with glitter. "I call these my Sparkle Cats," she informed Natie. "Don't they have pizzazz?"

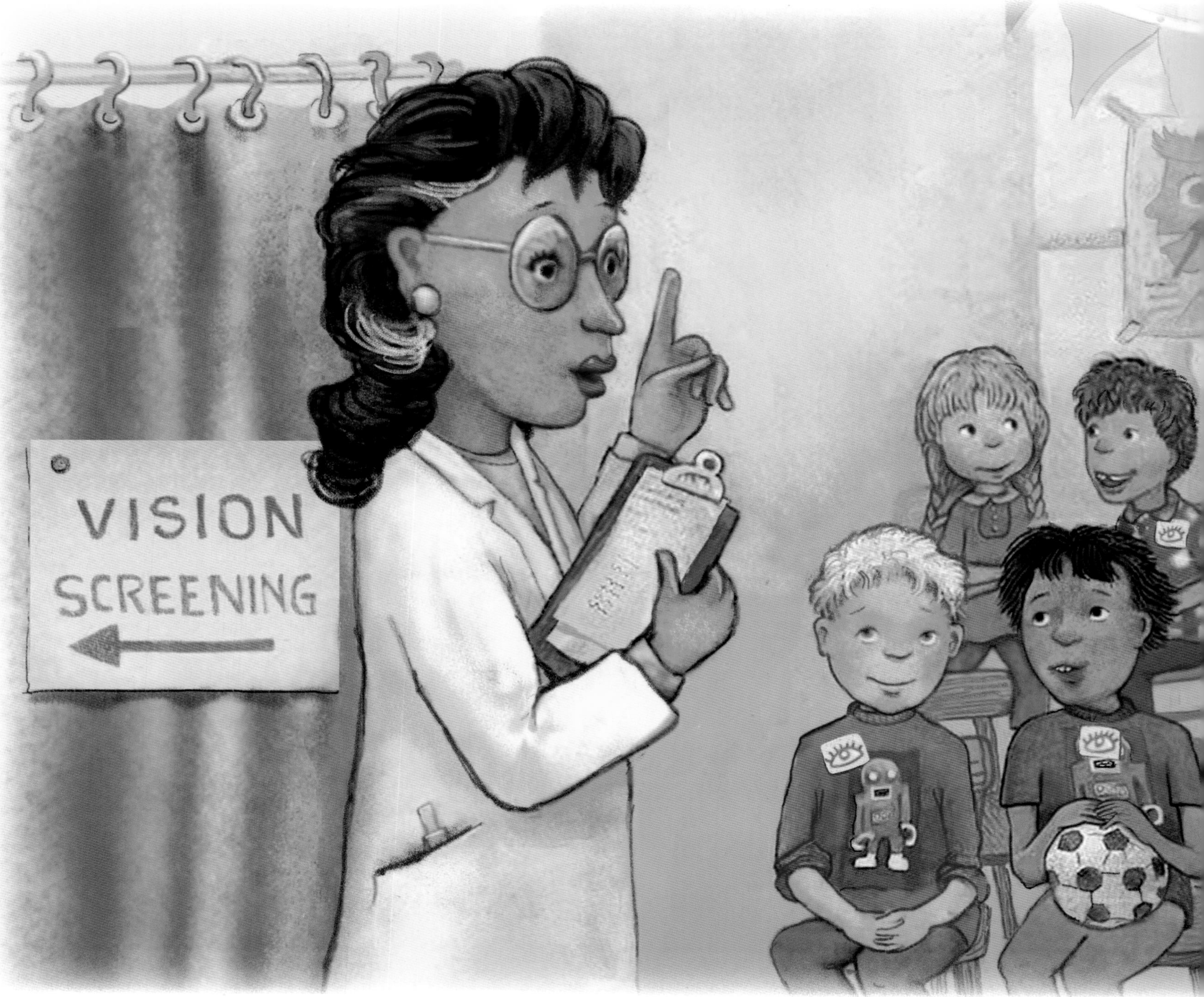
VISION
SCREENING

On Vision Screening Day, everyone waited their turn in the auditorium. Harris had his eyes checked first, then Gordon, then Fabio, then Doris.

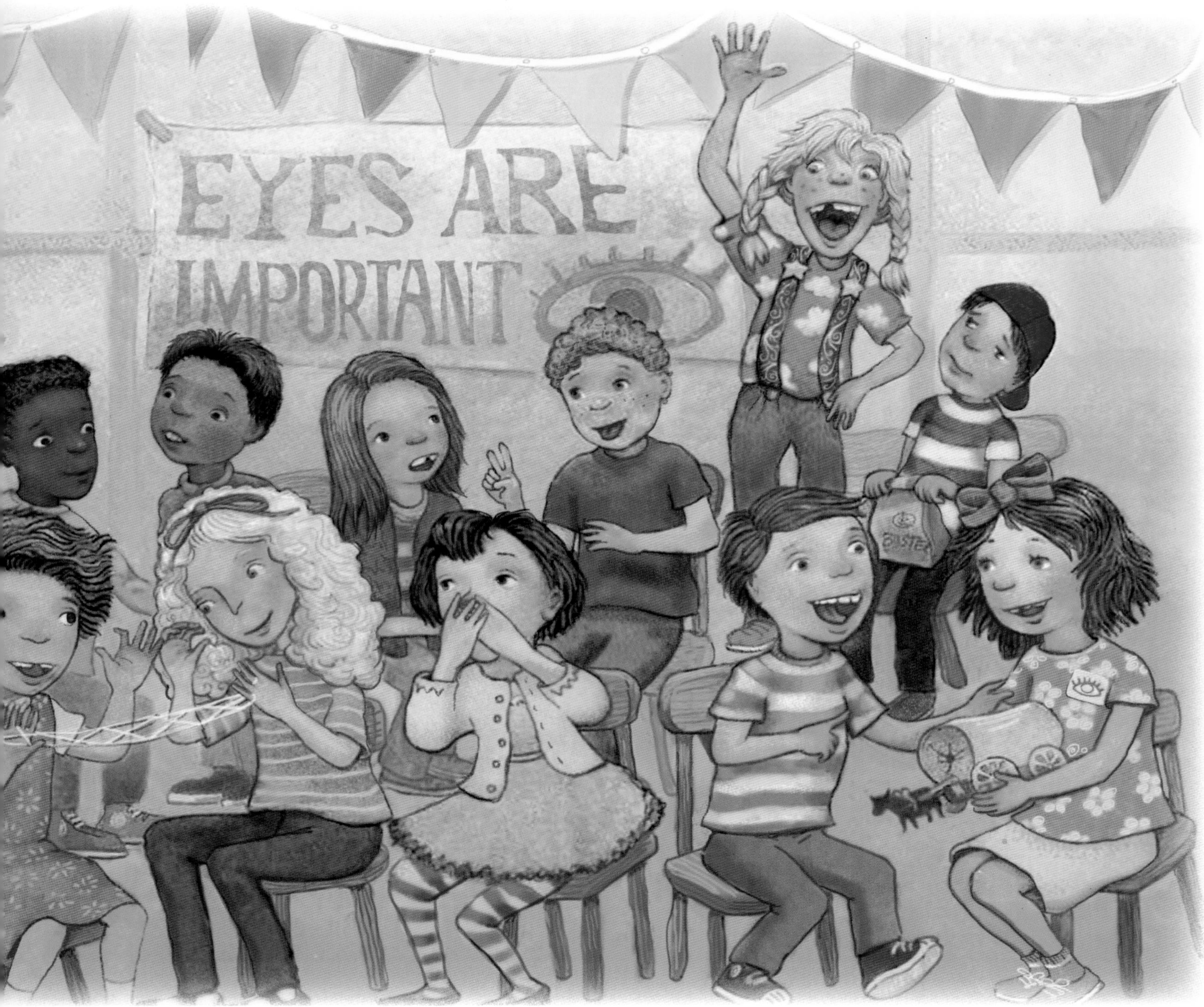
EYES ARE
IMPORTANT
BUSTER

When Carla's name was called, she leaped out of her chair.

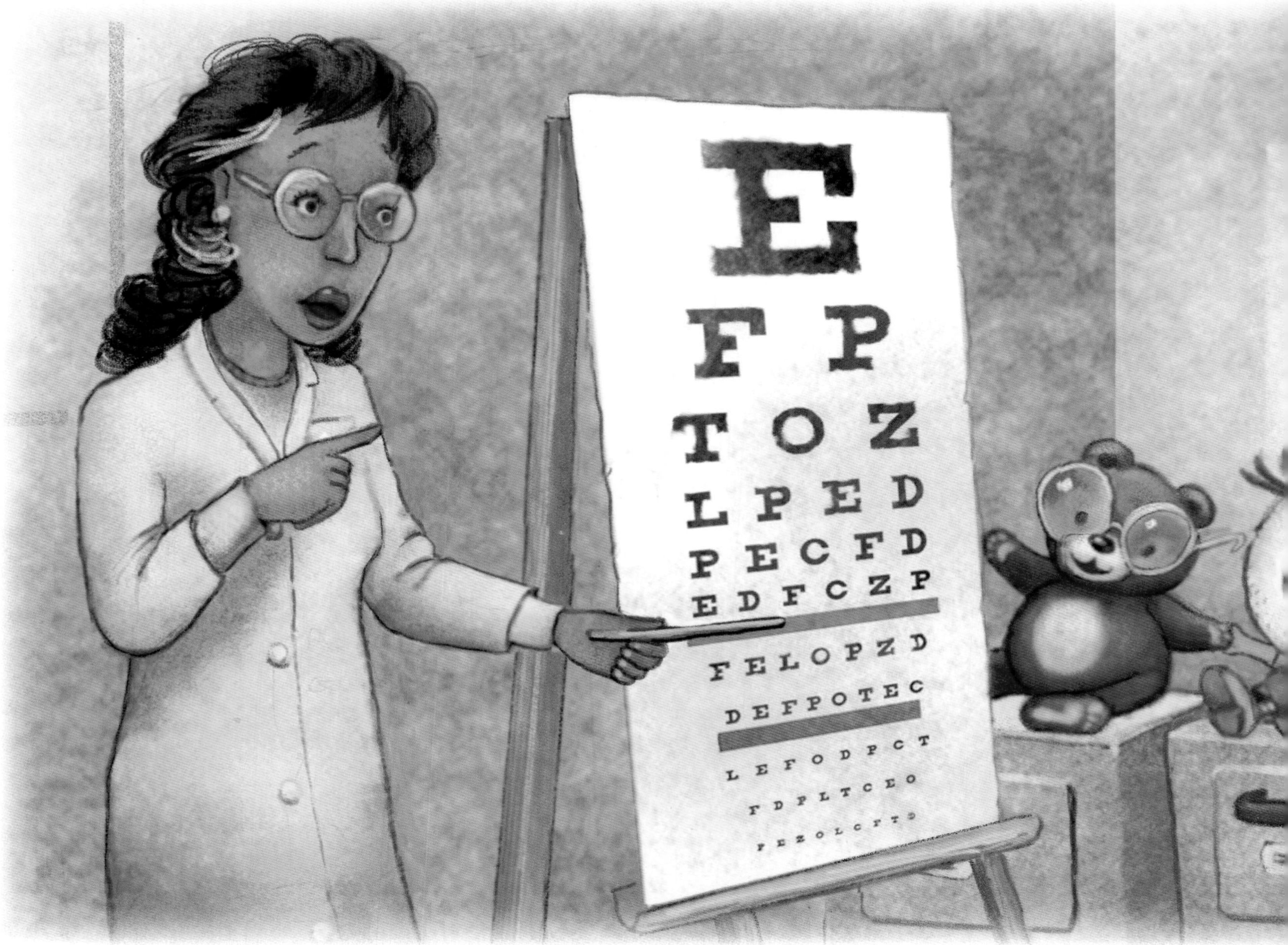
E
F P
T O Z
L P E D
P E C F D
E D F C Z P
F E L O P Z D
D E F P O T E C

"Hi, Carla!" said the nurse. "Please face the chart and cover your right eye. Now read this row of letters."
"EDFCZP," read Carla. "That was easy."
"Terrific," said the nurse. "Please continue."

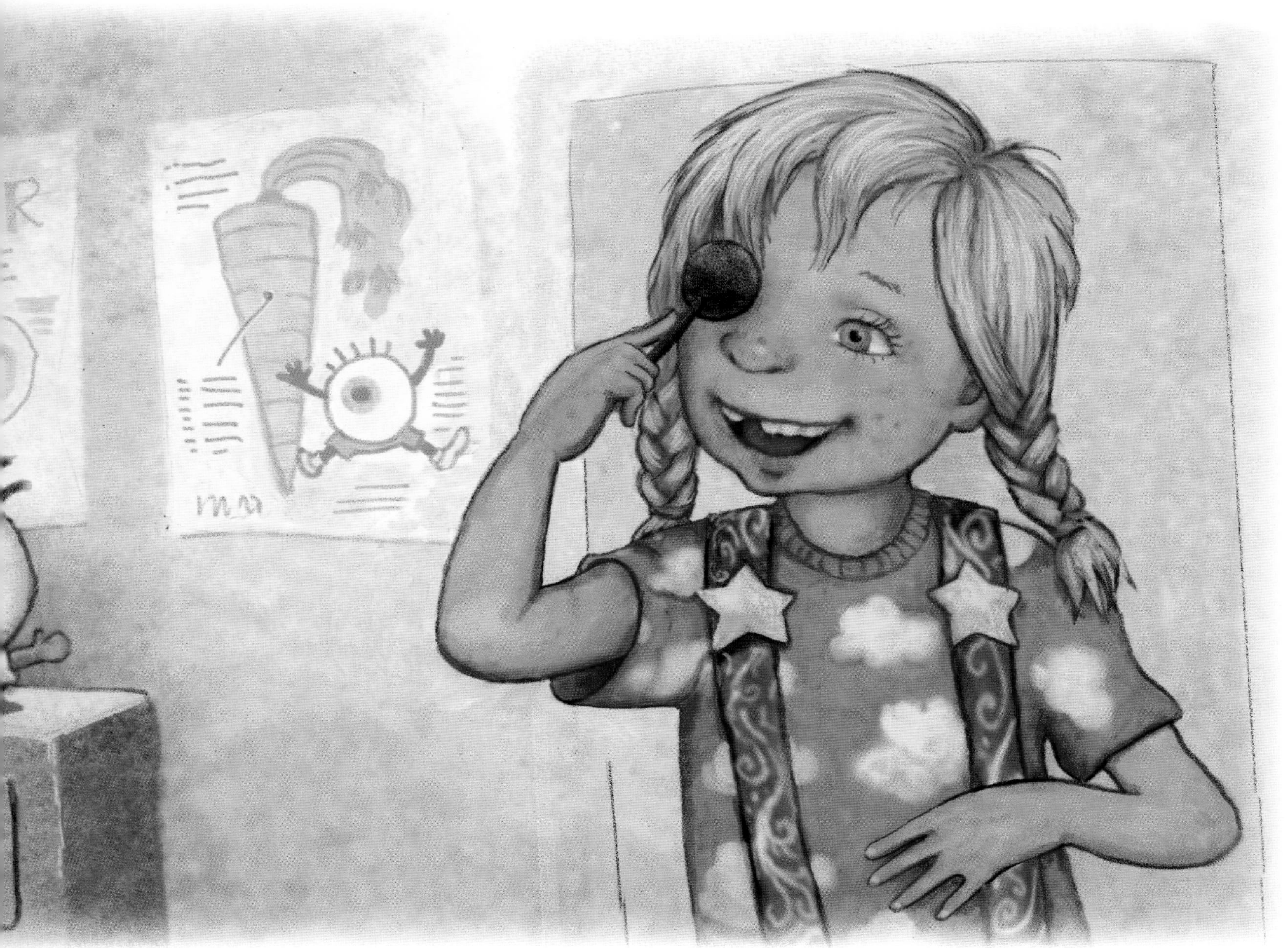

Carla read the next row and the next. "Hmm...it's getting tricky.
Is that a C or a G? I'll go with C."
"Great," said the nurse. "Now cover your left eye and we'll start again."
After a few more tests, the nurse handed Carla an eyeball sticker. "Nice job," she said.
"Thanks!" said Carla, and she skipped back to her seat.

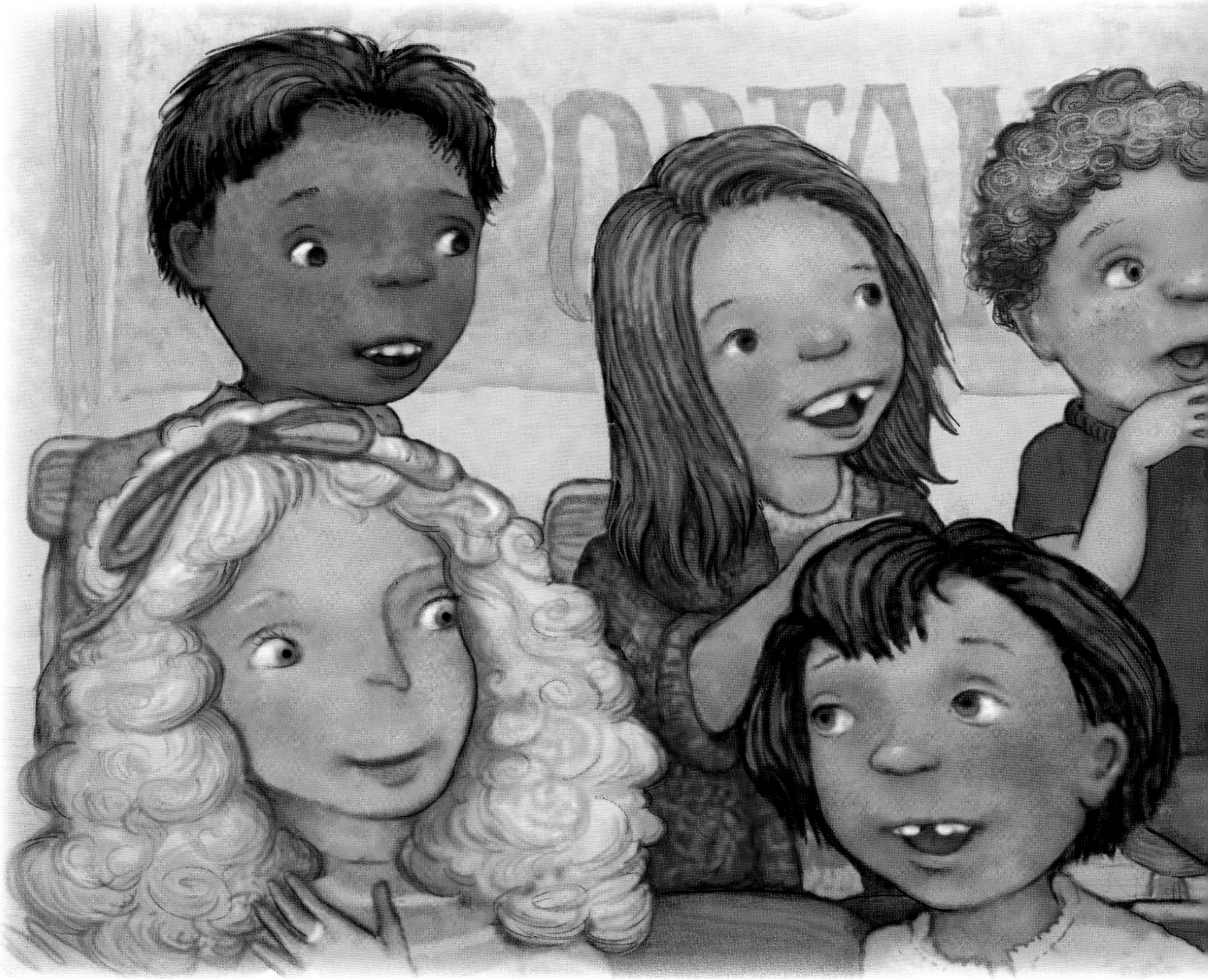

"What was it like?" asked Leslie. "Were you nervous?"
"No," said Carla, sticking the eyeball on her forehead. "It was fun."

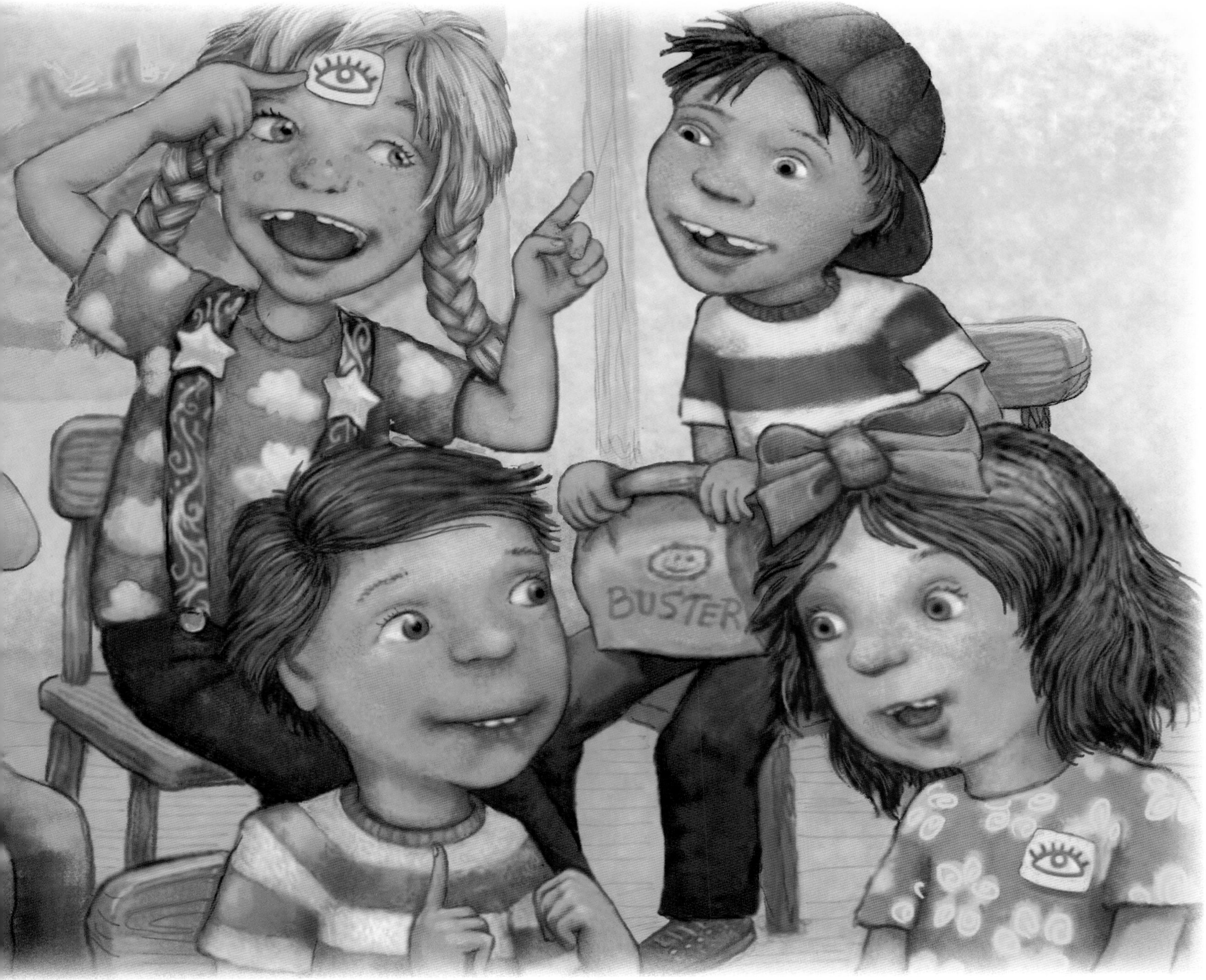
BUSTER

"How do you think you did?" asked Buster.
"Well, I wasn't sure about one of the letters. I hope that means I need glasses!"

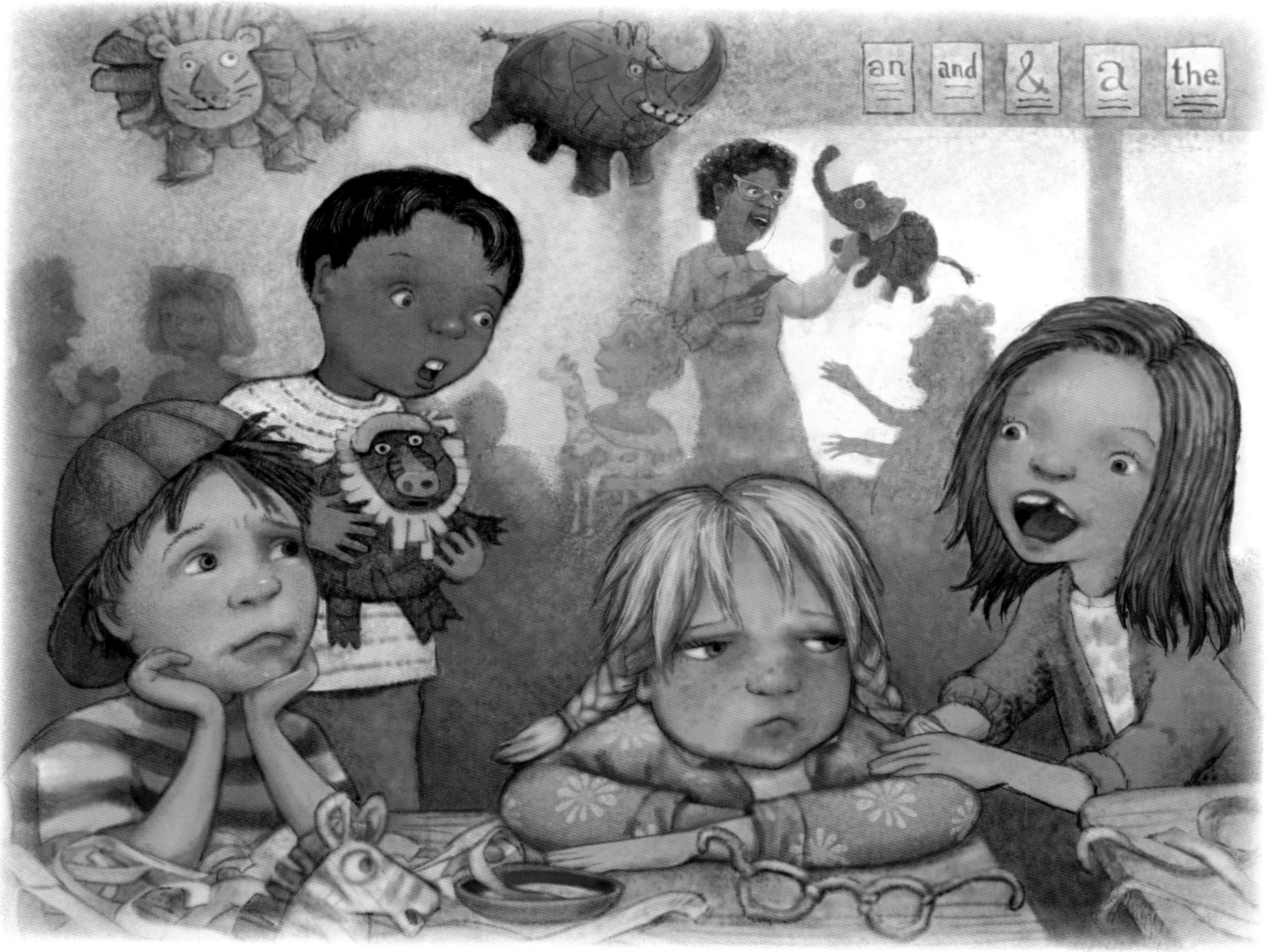
an
and
&
a
the

The next day, Carla and Buster were in bad moods.
"Why are you both so glum?" asked Leslie.
"I got the results of the screening," Carla explained. "I don't need glasses after all."
"And it looks like I do need glasses," grumbled Buster.
"You do?" asked Carla.
"You do?" asked Natie and Leslie.
"Probably. I'll know for sure when I get a full eye exam."

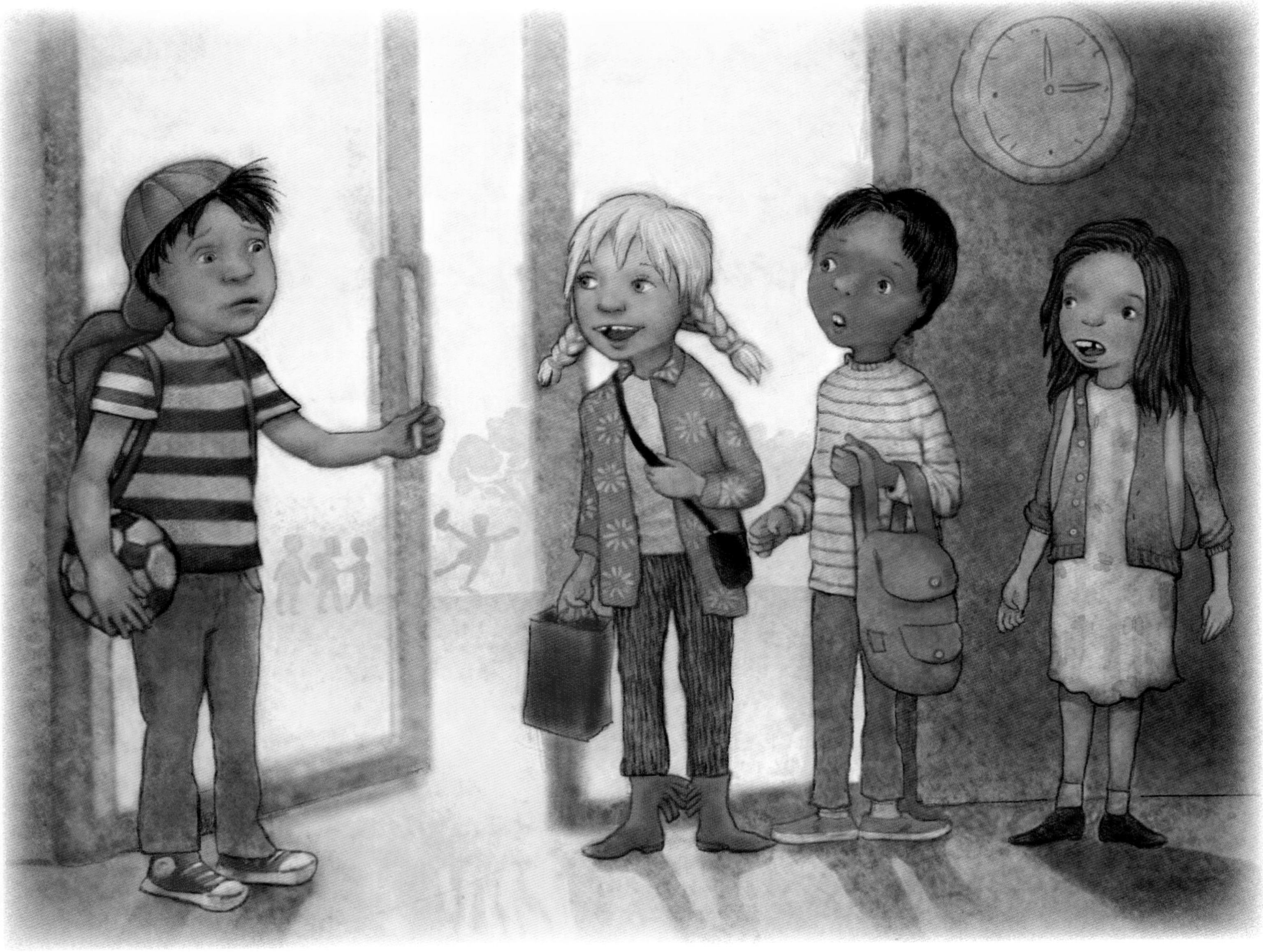

After school, Buster waited for his father to pick him up.
"I'm going to the optometrist now to get my eyes checked."
"Cool!" said Carla. "If my mother says it's okay, can I come with you? It sounds like fun!"
"It doesn't sound like fun to me," said Buster. "But sure."

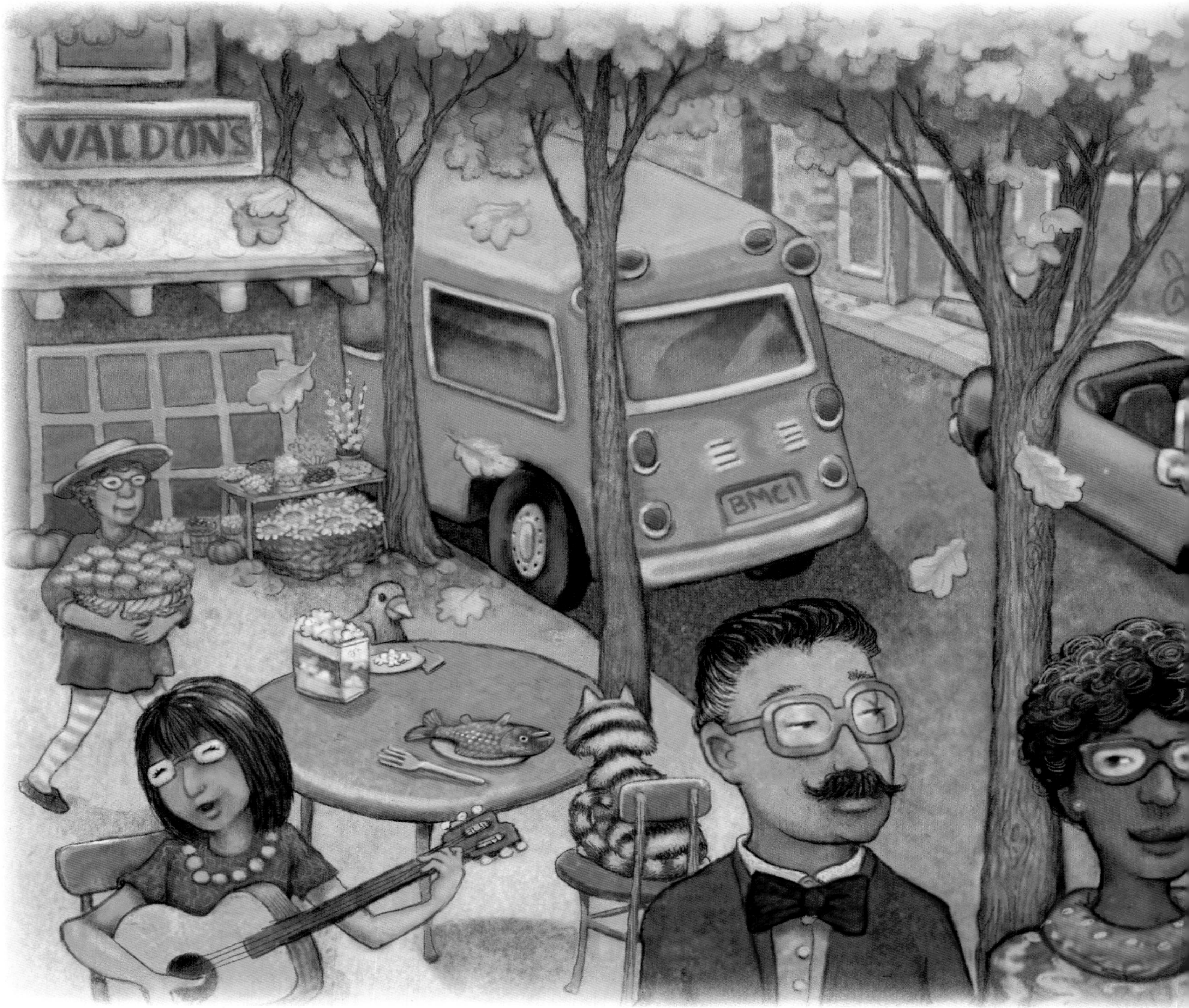
WALDON'S
BMC1

So Buster's dad drove Buster and Carla to Dr. Ollie's Eyewear.

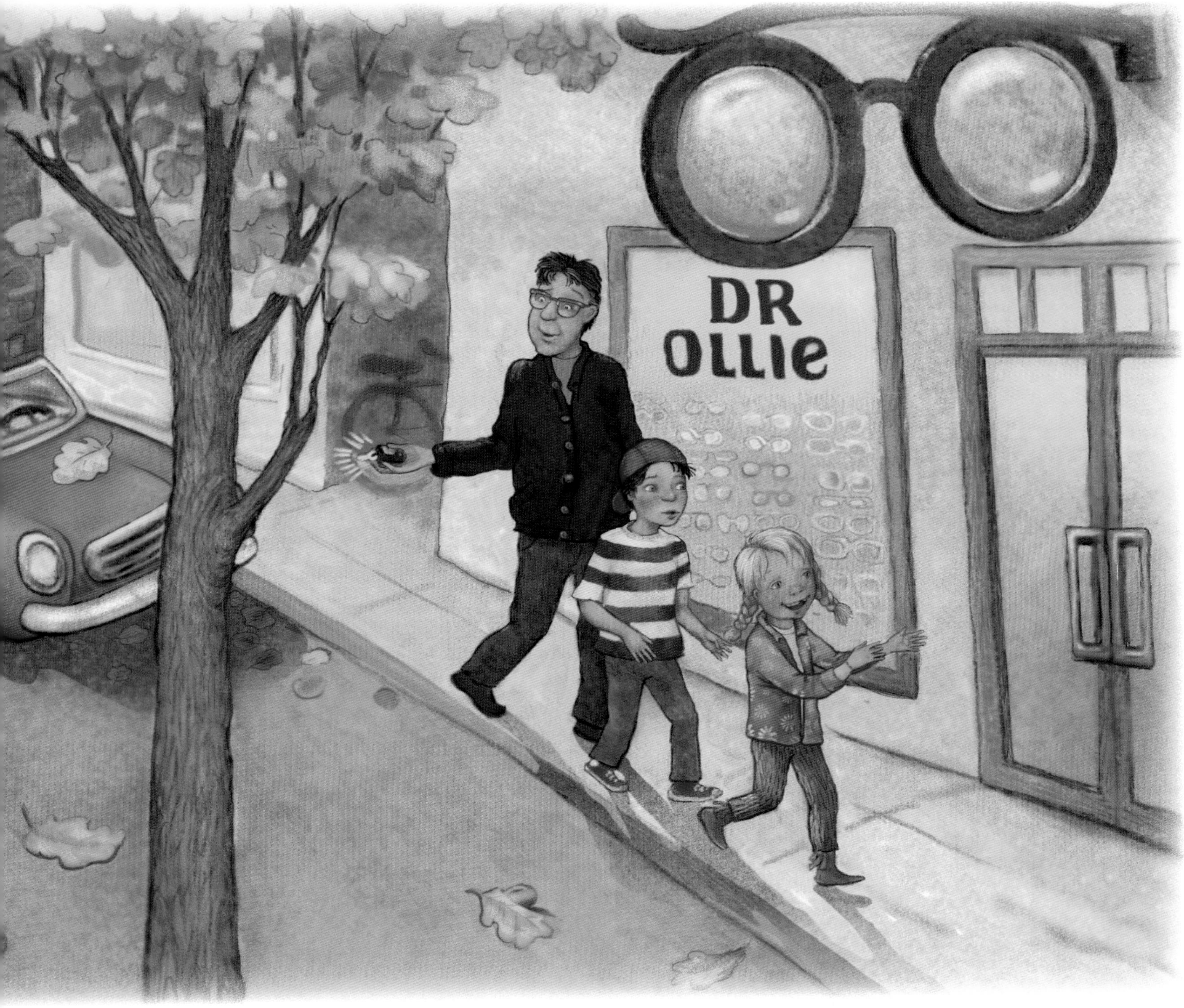
DR
OLLIE

“If you need glasses, I’ll help you pick out your frames!” said Carla, racing into the store.

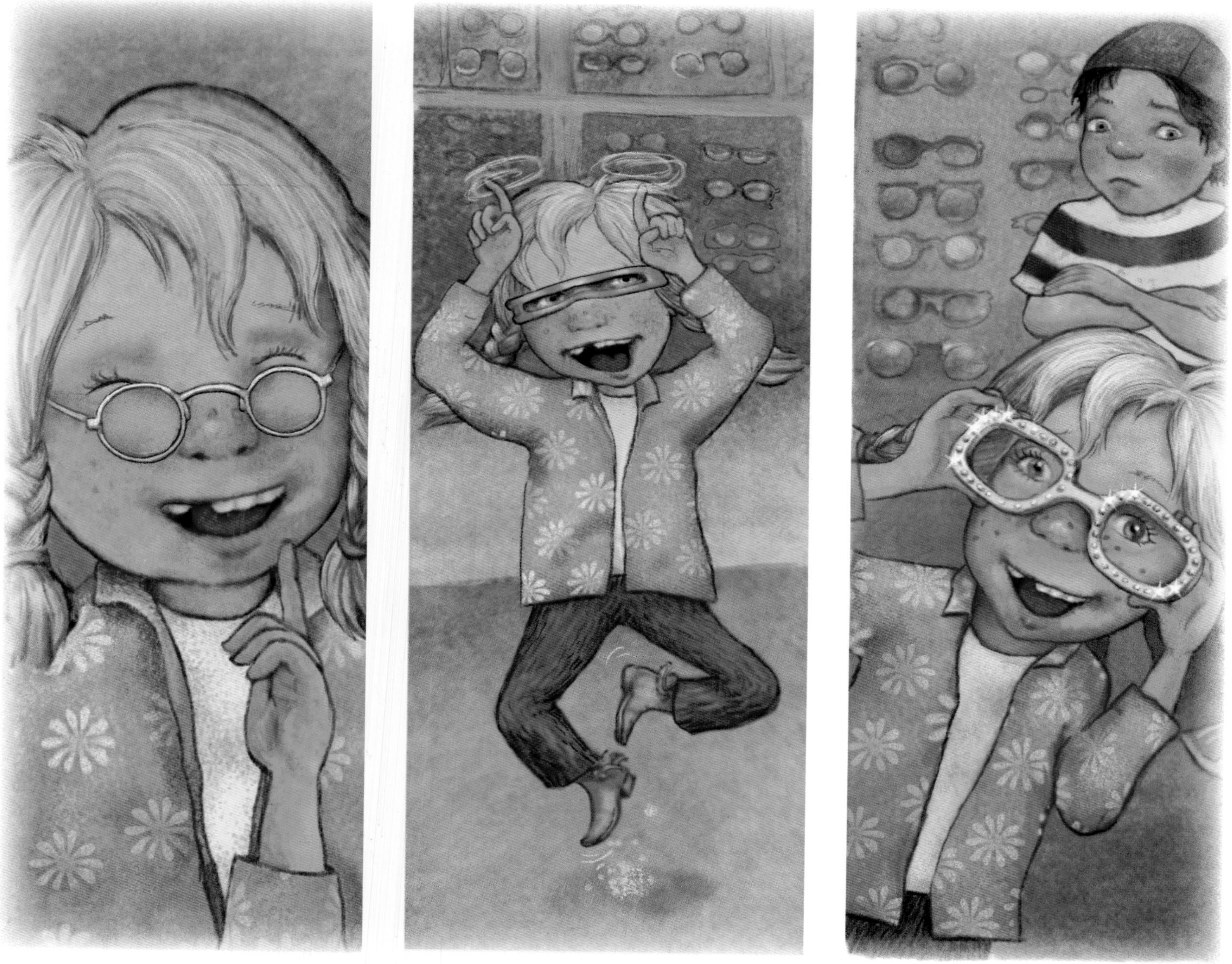

"Whoa!" Carla exclaimed, scanning the shelves. "There are so many colors and styles!"
She put on a pair of vintage wire frames. "Call me Professor Carla."
She tried on narrow, neon green frames. "I'm a space alien!"
Then she donned a pair with glimmering rhinestones. "Look, Buster! I'm a rock star!"

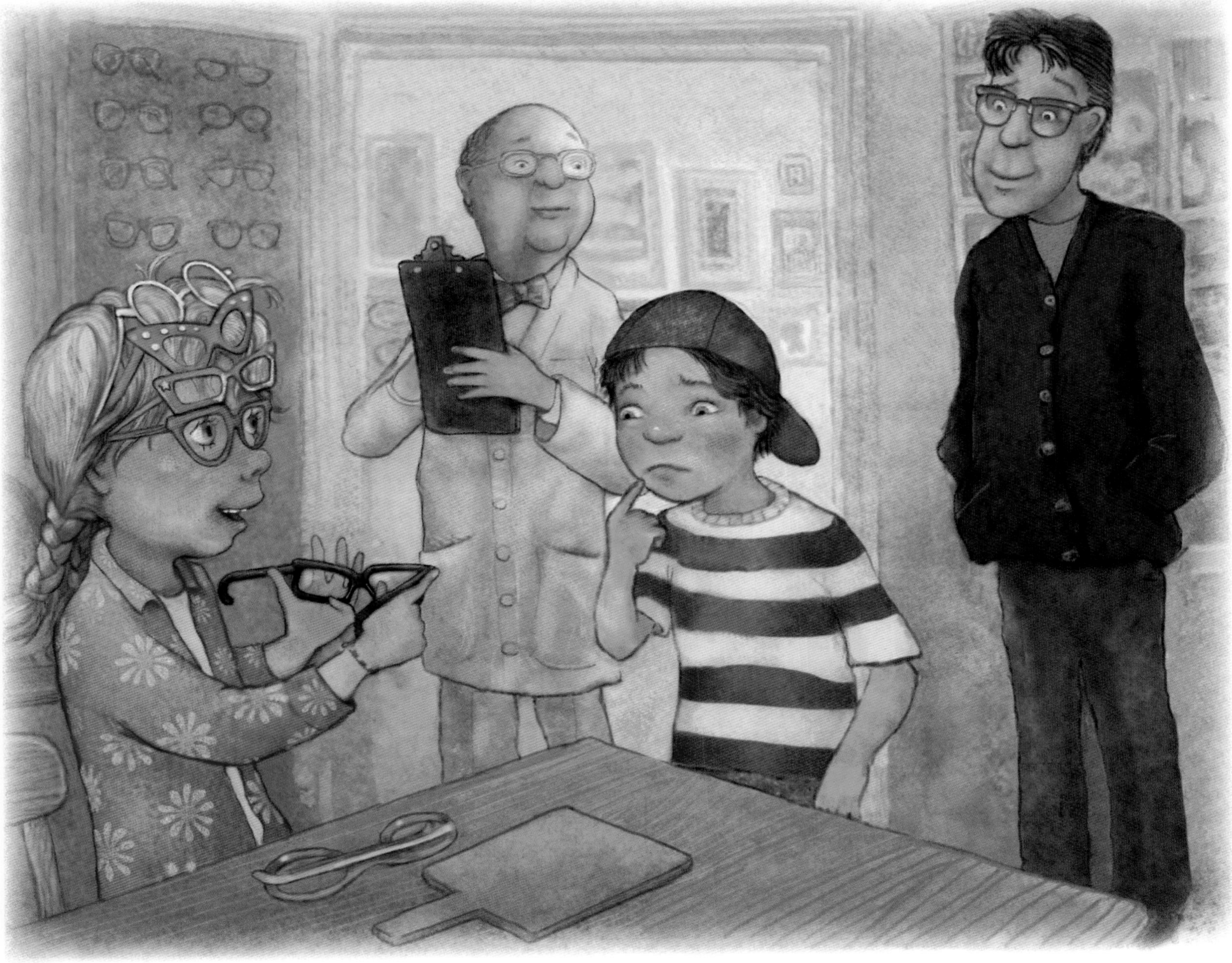

Buster didn't even crack a smile. He went into Dr. Ollie's office to get his eyes examined. When he came back out, he was frowning.
"It's official. I need glasses."

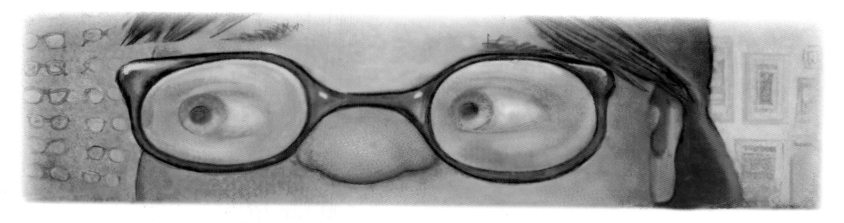

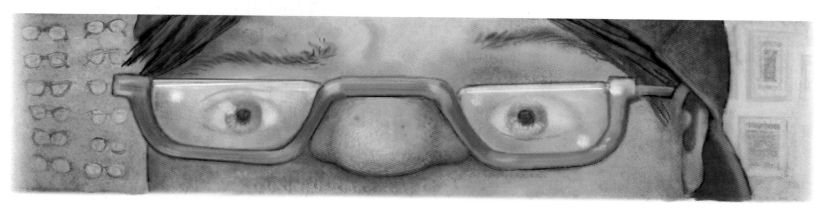

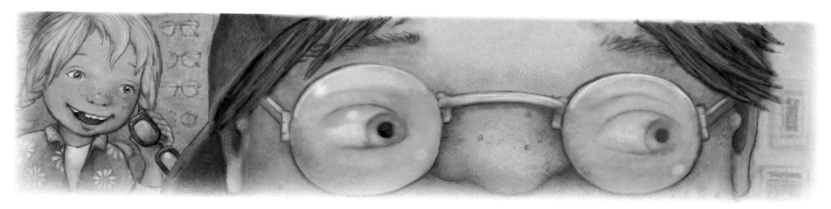

Dr. Ollie gave Buster some frames to try on. So did Buster's dad.
Then Carla handed Buster a pair. "Those look great on you!" she said.
"You look like a secret agent."
"I agree!" said Dr. Ollie.
"Me too!" said Buster's dad.

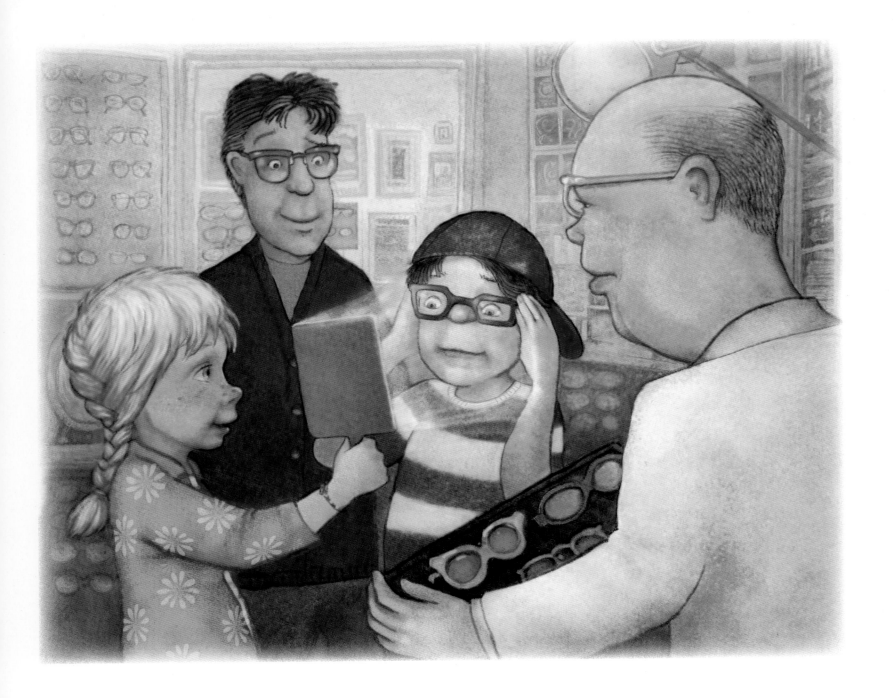

"What do you think, Buster?" asked Carla.

Buster looked in the mirror and sighed. "I guess they're okay."

So Buster's father ordered the glasses.

"They'll be ready in the morning," Dr. Ollie told them.

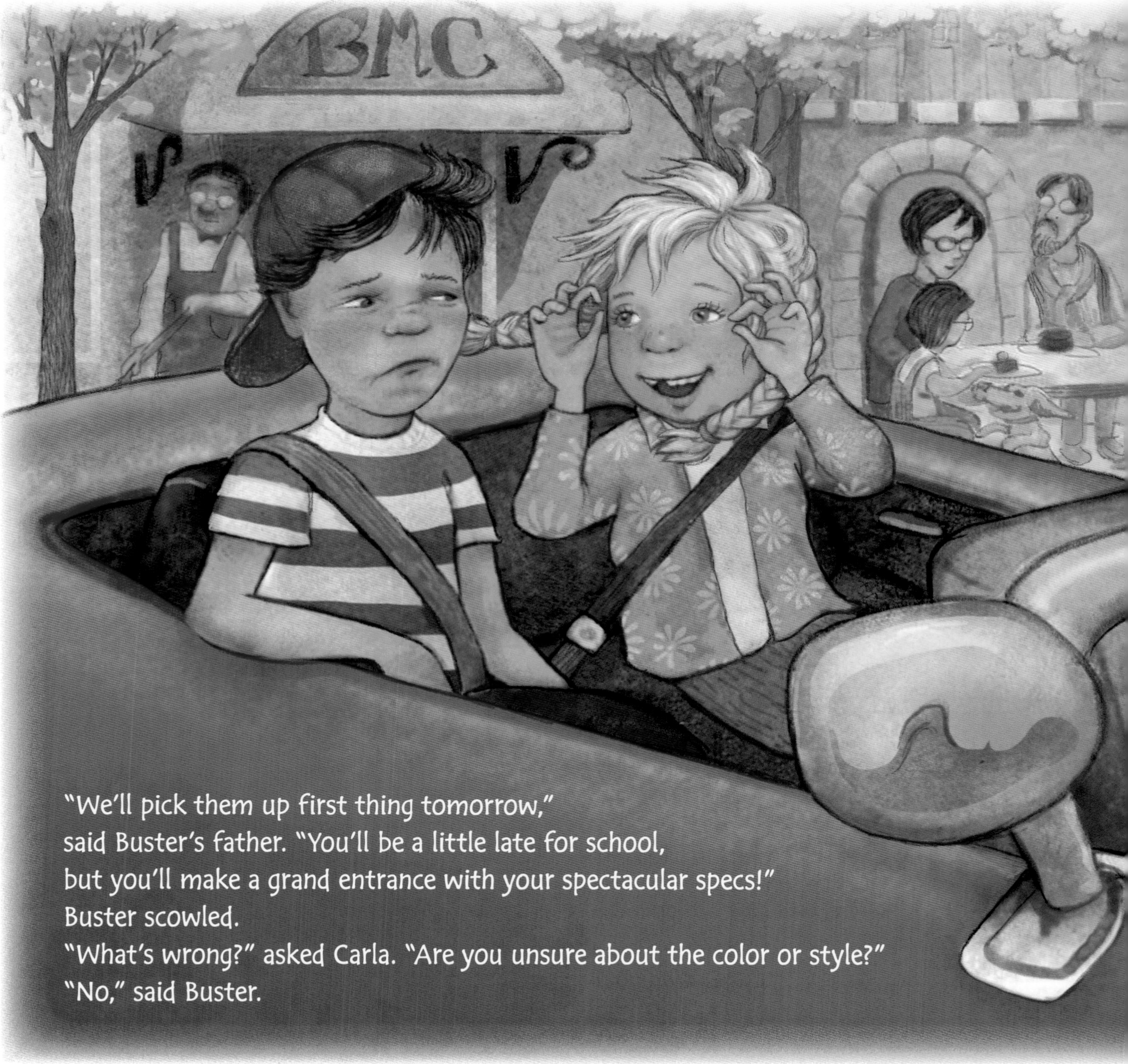
BMC

"We'll pick them up first thing tomorrow,"
said Buster's father. "You'll be a little late for school,
but you'll make a grand entrance with your spectacular specs!"
Buster scowled.
"What's wrong?" asked Carla. "Are you unsure about the color or style?"
"No," said Buster.

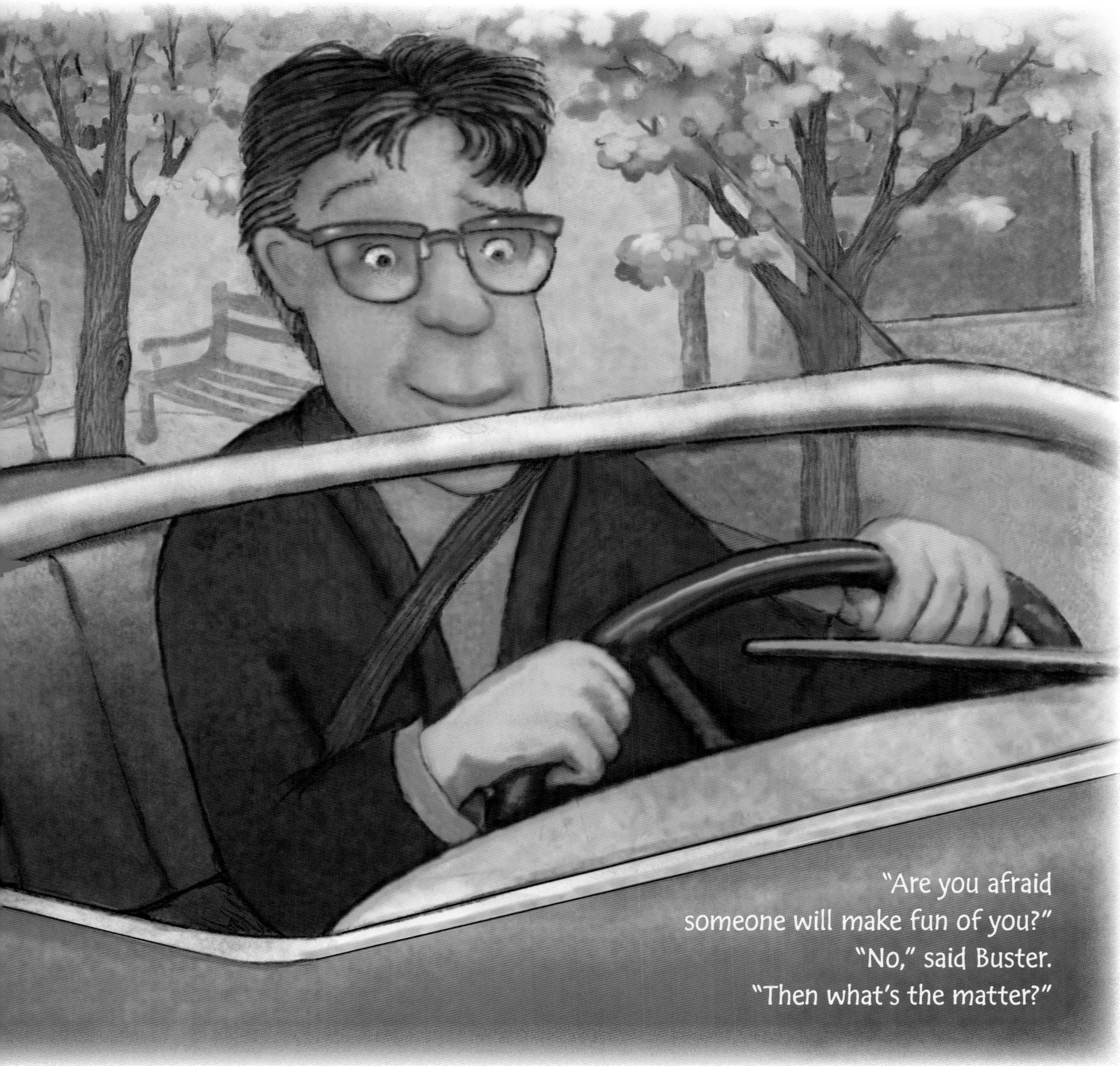

"Are you afraid
someone will make fun of you?"
"No," said Buster.
"Then what's the matter?"

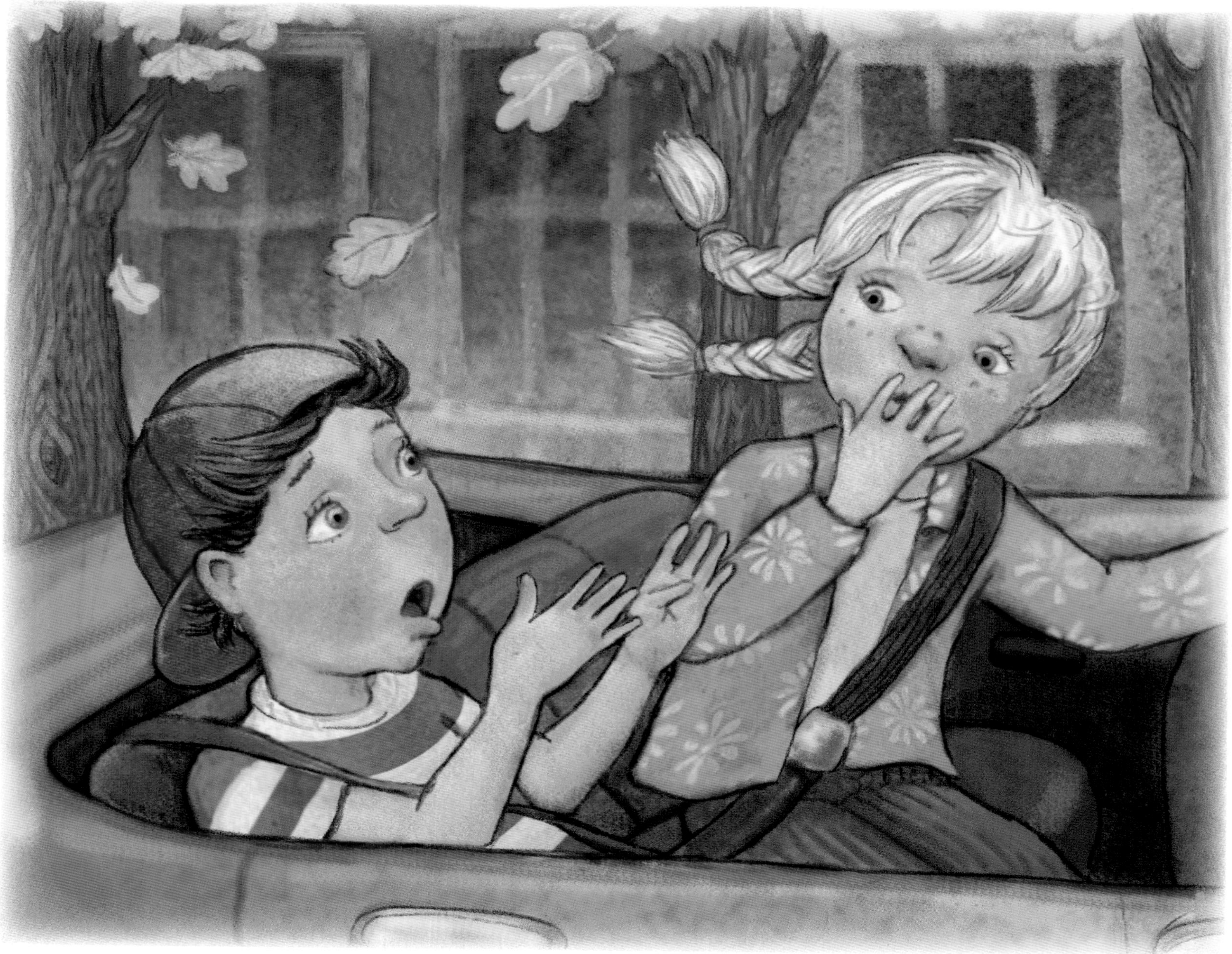

"Well," said Buster, "you know how you like to be different?"
Carla nodded.
"I'm the opposite. I like to blend in. But tomorrow, when I walk into class, I'm going to stand out. Everyone will be looking at me."
"I get it," sighed Carla. "I wish there was something I could do."

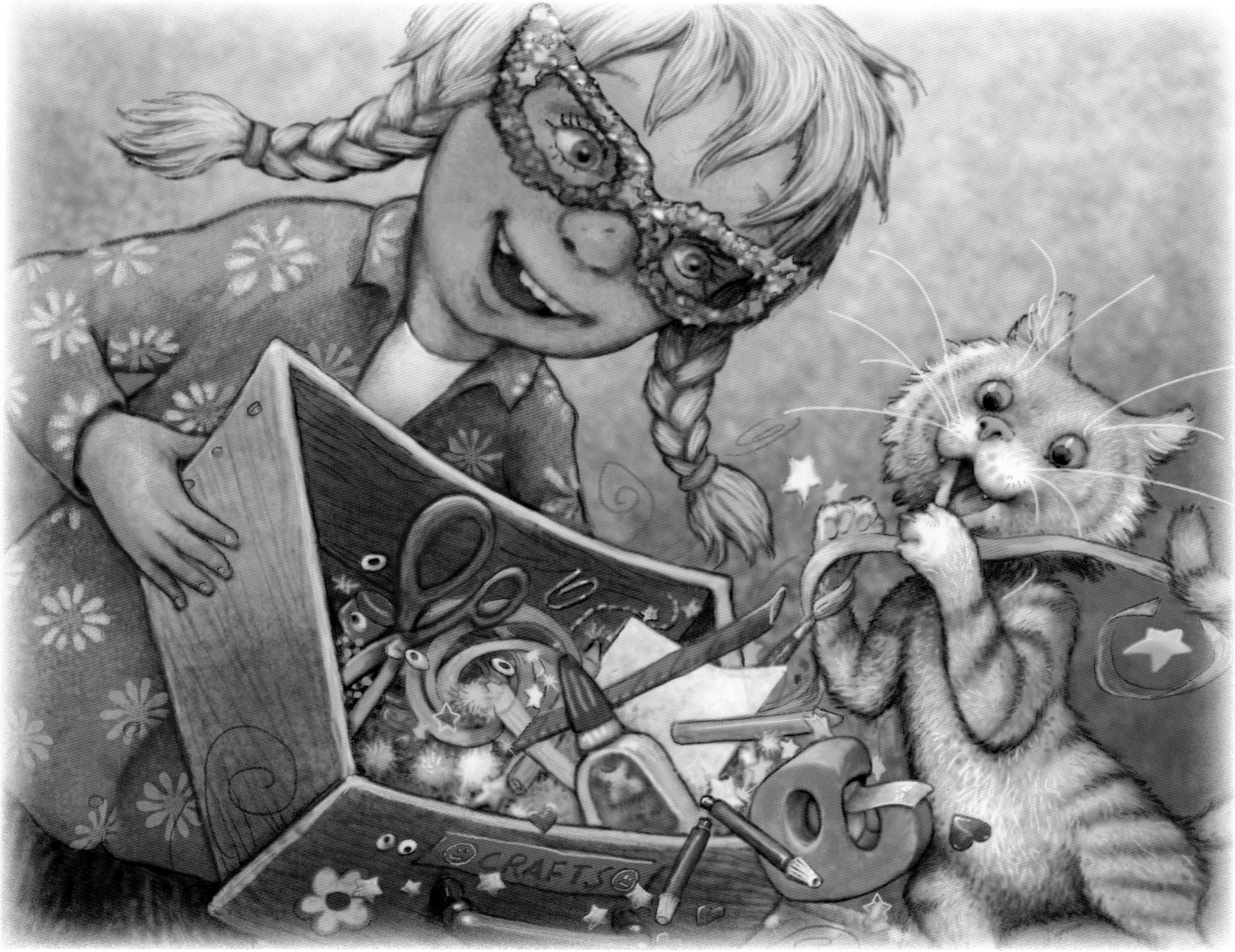
CRAFTS

When Carla got home, she raced to her room, put on her Sparkle Cats, and started brainstorming ways to help Buster.

"That's it!" she cried.

Carla dumped everything out of her crafts drawer.

She cut. She glued. She bent. She shaped. She painted.

Then she packed everything up in a box.

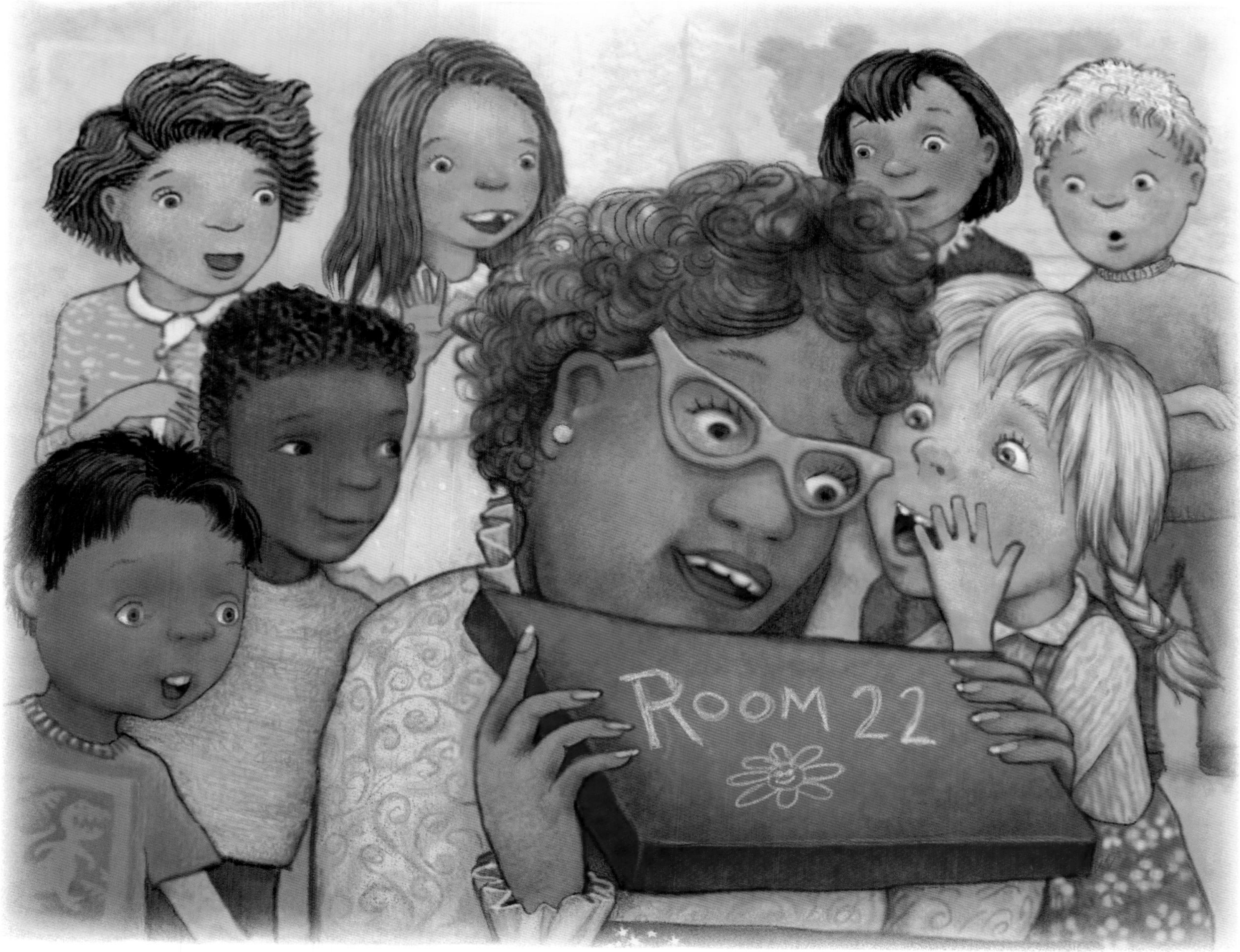
ROOM 22

The next morning, Carla handed the box to Ms. Pimento and whispered something in her ear. Ms. Pimento peeked inside, smiled and nodded. "Take one and pass it down," Carla announced to everyone. There were oohs and aahs and lots of giggling.

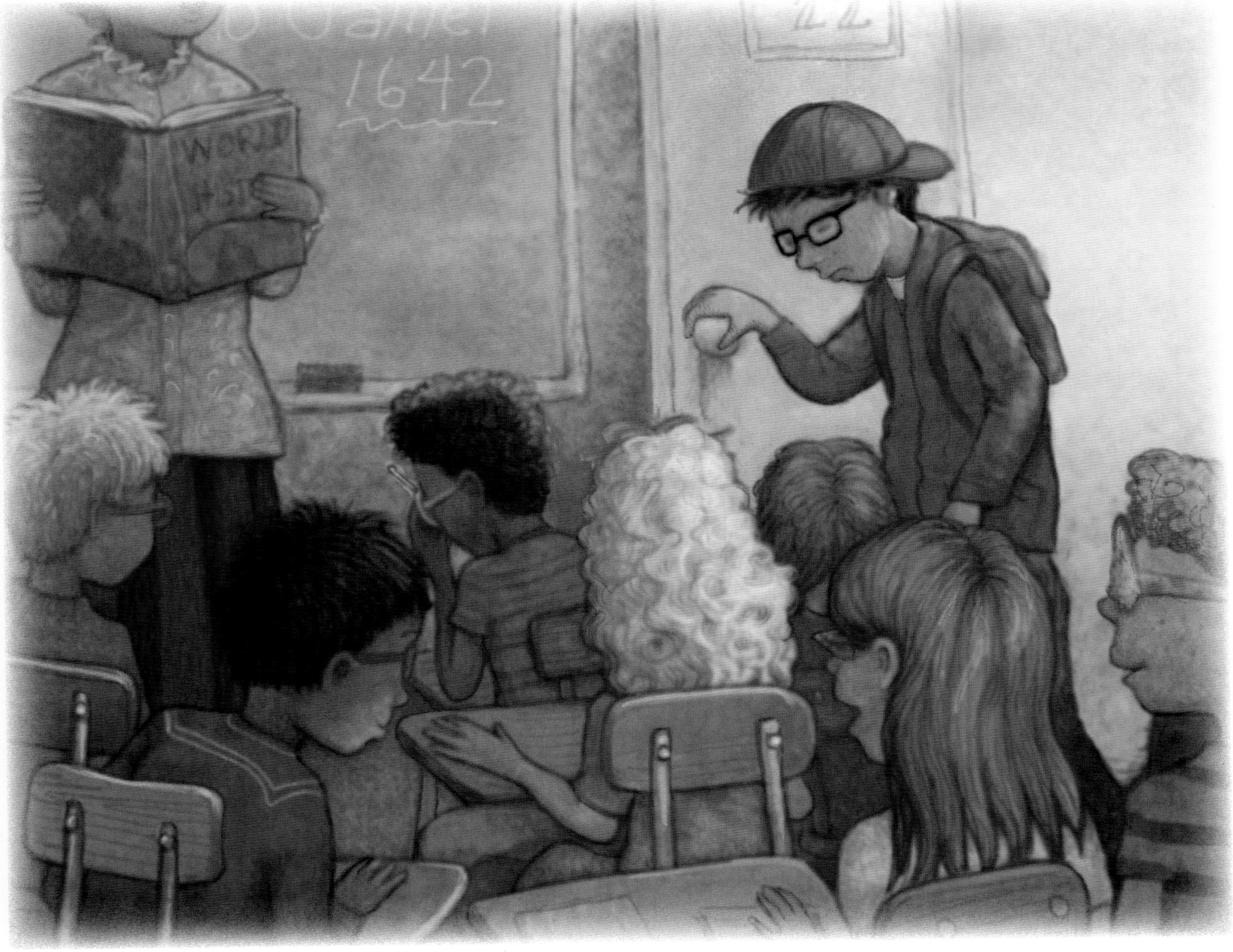
1642

The class had finally settled down when the doorknob turned and the door opened slightly. Buster inched his way into the classroom, eyes on the floor.

"Hey, Buster!" called Carla.

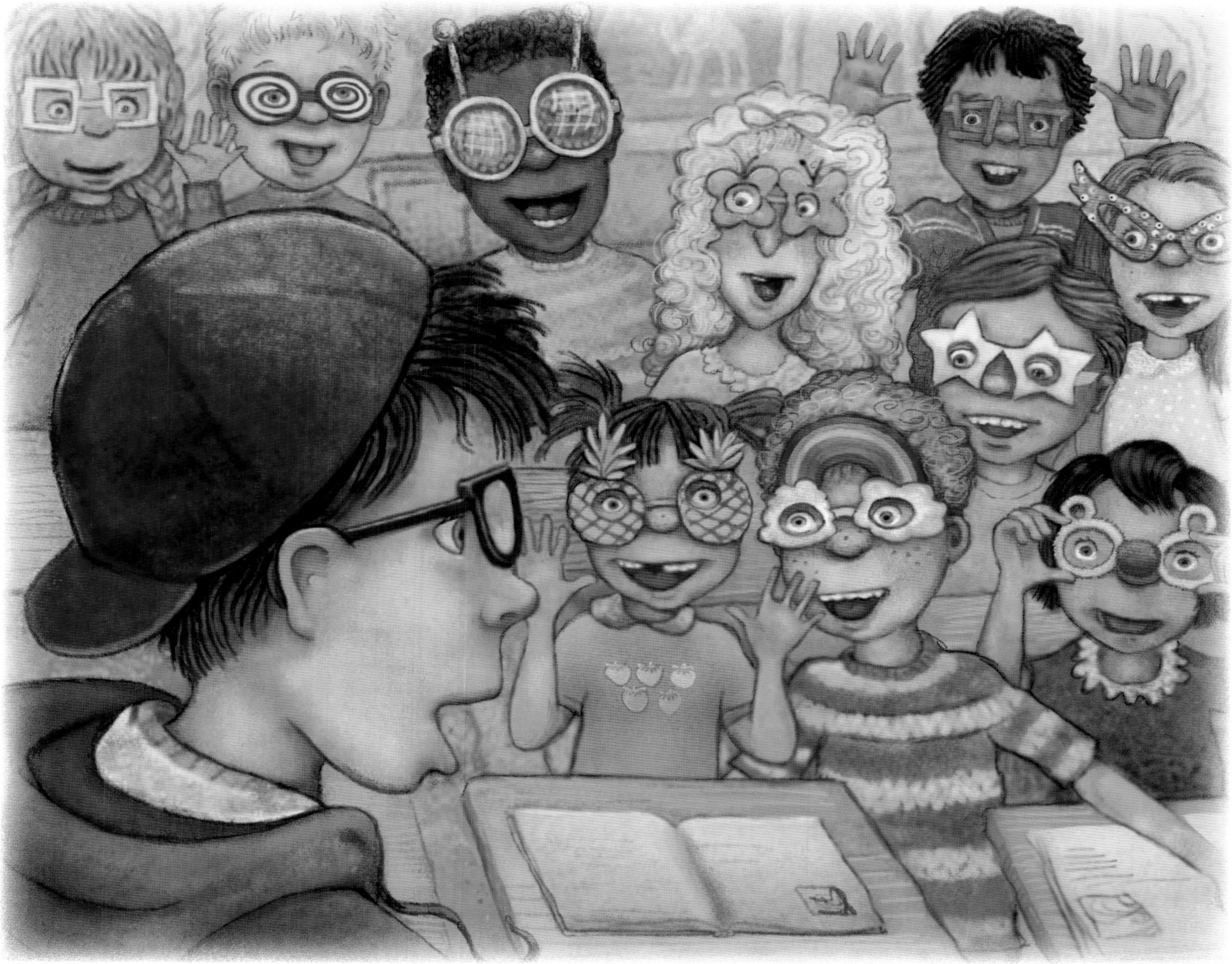

Buster lifted his head. Looking back at him were rows of smiling faces.
And on each face was a pair of glasses – Carla's glasses!
Buster smiled. Then he burst out laughing.

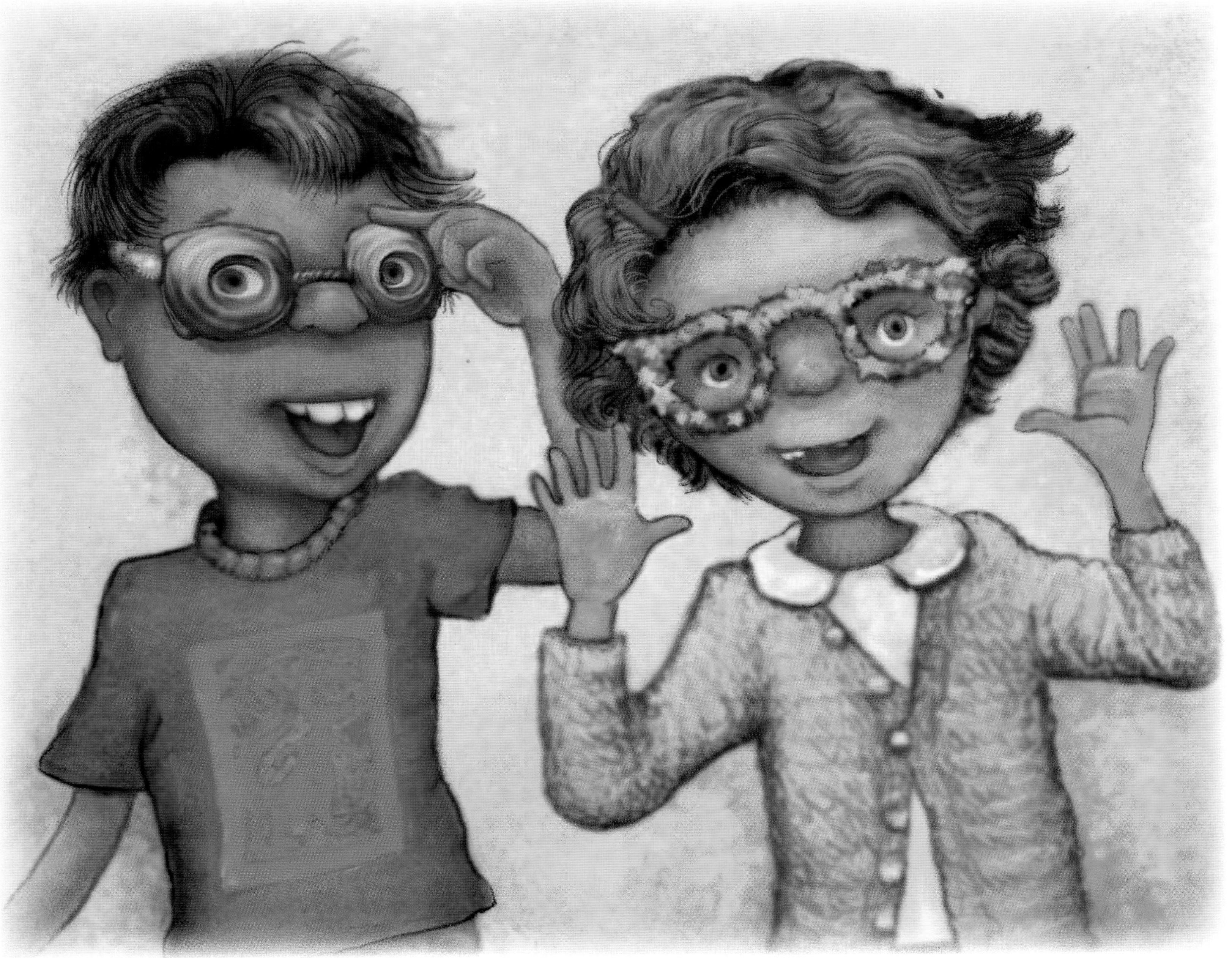

"Your glasses are cool, Buster!" said Natie, peering through egg carton frames. "But mine are egg-cellent!"
"And look at mine!" shouted Darcy. "They're so blingy!"

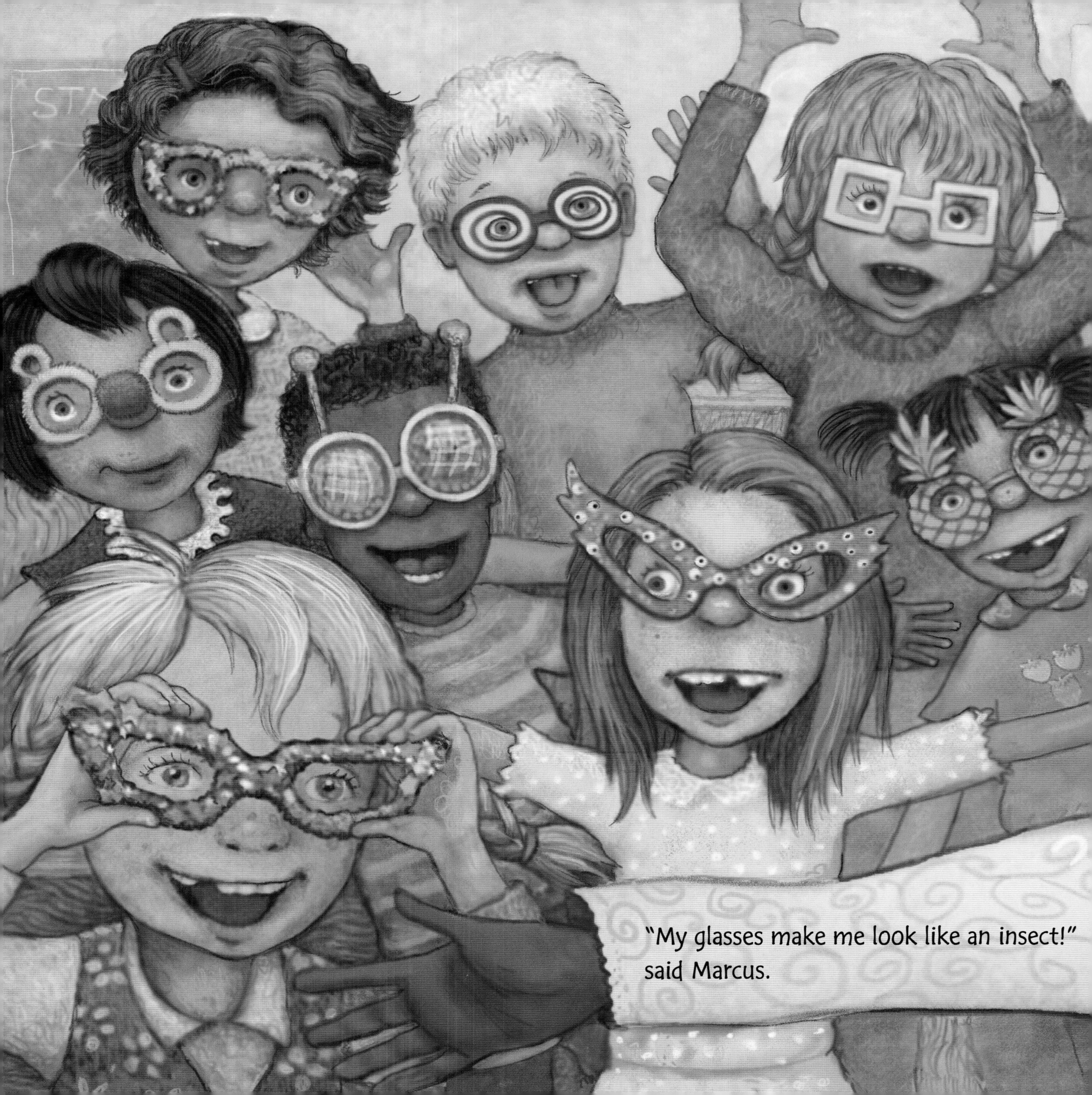

"My glasses make me look like an insect!" said Marcus.

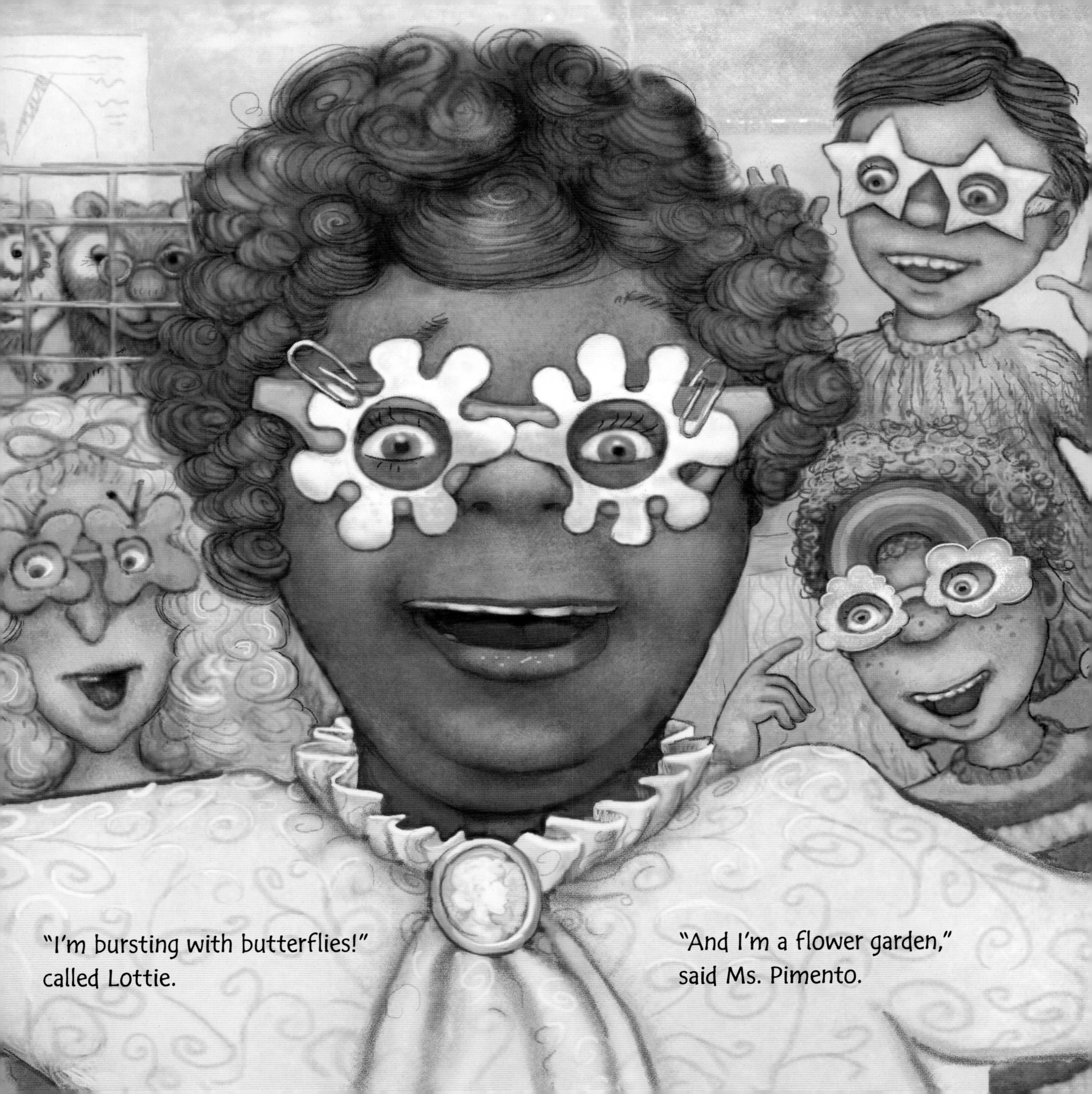

"I'm bursting with butterflies!" called Lottie.

"And I'm a flower garden," said Ms. Pimento.

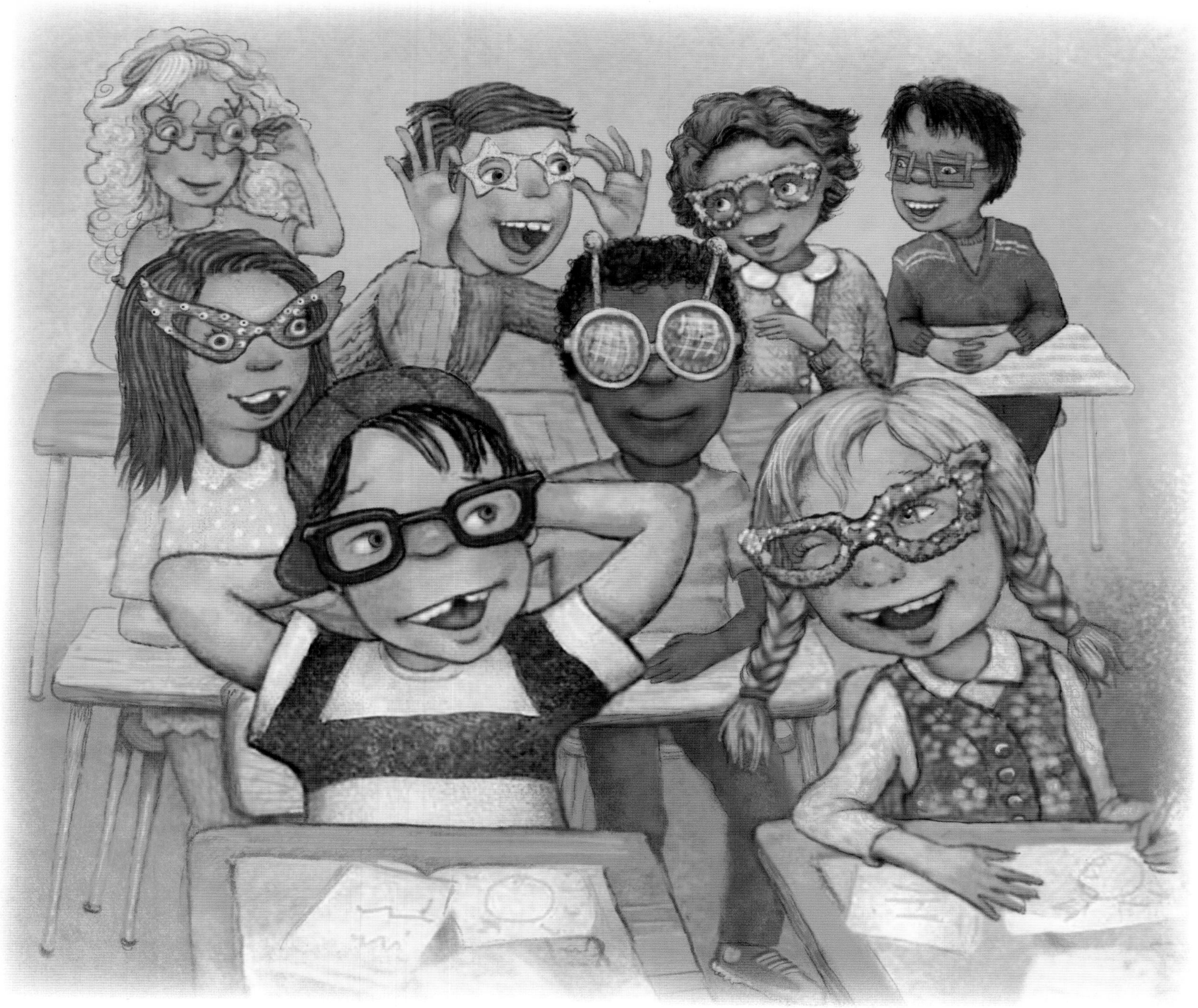

As everyone compared glasses, Carla turned to Buster.
"See? You don't stand out after all."
"That's for sure!" said Buster. "Thanks to you, I blend right in!"

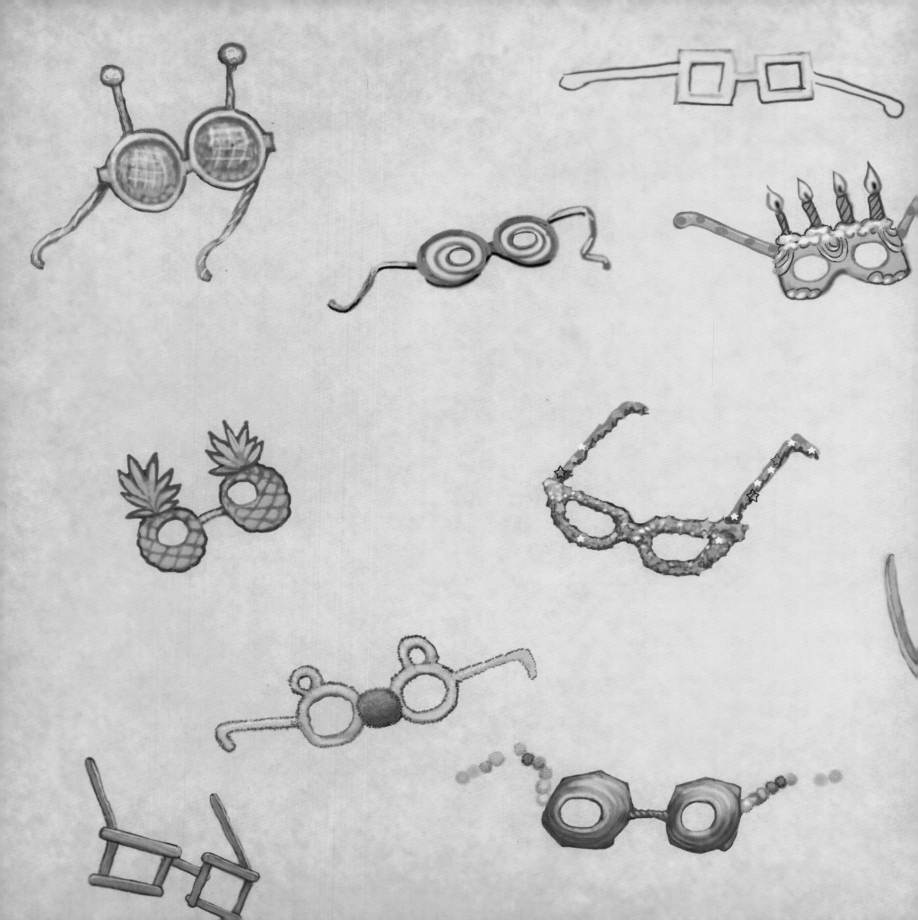